IN THE LOOP

HANNAH MONTANA

IN THE LOOP

by Suzanne Harper

Based on the series created by Michael Poryes and Rich Correll & Barry O'Brien

Disney Press
New York

IN THE
LOOP

For Renee Sanders

Printed in the United States of America
First Edition
1 3 5 7 9 10 8 6 4 2

Library of Congress Control Number on file.
ISBN 978-1-4231-1662-2

For more Disney Press fun, visit www.disneybooks.com
Visit DisneyChannel.com

Reinforced binding

Designed by Roberta Pressel

Chapter One

If you climb in the saddle, be ready for the ride.
—Traditional cowboy saying

"So what do you say?" An announcer's voice boomed through the auditorium of the Surfside Arena, where thousands of fans had just danced and sung along to a two-hour Hannah Montana concert. "Do you want"— the announcer paused for dramatic effect— "*one more song from Hannah Montana?*"

The audience screamed so loudly that Miley Stewart, who was standing backstage, thought she could see the air shimmer.

She took several deep breaths to slow down her heart rate. The announcer, a short, balding man who clearly loved his job, looked over and held up three fingers. He raised one eyebrow.

Miley nodded. She had just done two encores, but she still felt full of energy. She started tapping her foot, ready and eager to run back into the spotlight.

The announcer held the microphone back up to his mouth. "I'm not sure I heard that!" he shouted. "Let me ask once more: do you want Hannah Montana to come out here and sing again or not?"

The noise sounded the way a jet engine might, Miley thought. If you were standing one foot away. And if the engine were chanting, "Han-*nah*! Han-*nah*! Han-*nah*!"

"All right, then!" he yelled into the mike. "Here she is! The one! The only! *Hannah Montana!*"

Then he nodded and pointed his finger at Miley. She danced back onstage, her heart racing again, this time from pure joy.

☆   ☆   ☆

Fifteen minutes later, Miley dashed backstage and into her dressing room. She was still breathless from that last encore, not to mention the sprint from the stage to the dressing room.

"Wow!" she said, grabbing a bottle of water from a table piled high with bowls of candy, platters of sandwiches, and cans of soda. "That was a blast, but now I'm dryer than a dirt road in August." She took a big swig of water and threw herself into a chair. "Is it midnight yet? I'm ready to turn back into regular Miley for a while."

She flipped her long blond hair over her shoulder impatiently. When she was Miley Stewart, a normal high school girl, she loved being able to put on the wig that transformed her into Hannah Montana, international pop star. But sometimes—like right now, after performing her heart out under hot stage lights for more than two hours—she couldn't wait to put on her old blue jeans and feel cool air on her own brown hair.

"Hold it, Cinderella," said her best friend, Lilly Truscott. "Let me live vicariously through you for just a little longer." She did the pleading-puppy-dog eyes that always won Miley over. "You know you're my only connection to the glamorous life."

"Oh, yeah, because backstage dressing rooms are decorated in such a sophisticated style," Miley said, rubbing at a worn spot on the chair's drab brown upholstery.

"I'll take what I can get," Lilly said. As always when she accompanied Hannah, Lilly was disguised as Lola Luftnagle, a rich socialite who was also Hannah Montana's best friend. As part of her look, Lilly had collected wigs in a variety of different colors; tonight's was streaked bright blue, raspberry pink, and neon yellow. People had to shield their eyes when she stood under a strong light.

Lilly walked over to the snack table. "Free sodas and plastic cups already filled with ice! And look, we even get those little plastic sticks you can put in your free soda after you've poured it over the free ice!"

Miley tilted her head to one side and pretended to think this over. Then she nodded. "You're right," she said. "This is the life."

Just then, the dressing-room door opened and two more people entered the room. That is, Miley thought, one person—her other best friend, Oliver Oken—and one annoying, irritating and subhuman creature, also known as her older brother, Jackson.

"Great concert, Miley," Oliver said. "You were awesome!"

She smiled happily. "Aww, thanks so—"

"Hey, cool, they brought in more chips!" Oliver interrupted as he made a beeline for the snack table.

"And extra candy bars," Jackson said, grabbing a handful and stuffing them in his pocket. He rummaged behind a bowl of chips. "And look! Doughnut holes!"

"Is that *all* I am to you people?" Miley

asked, pretending to be miffed. "Just a way for you to score free junk food?"

"Yeah, pretty much," Jackson replied, stuffing another handful of mini candy bars into his other pocket. "Anyway, it's your fault we're starving. If you hadn't kept going back onstage, over and over and over again—"

"It's called an encore, Jackson," she snapped. Then she smiled smugly at him. "What can I say, my fans can't get enough of me."

"Oh, like you weren't chomping at the bit to go back onstage," Jackson said. He struck a pose, pretending to be Hannah Montana, and said in a high-pitched voice, "What? You want to hear li'l ol' me sing again? Well, hey, how 'bout I sing *five* more songs, as long as I'm hogging the spotlight?"

"That is so unfair," Lilly said.

Miley shot her an appreciative glance. "Aww, thanks, Lil—"

"Miley only sang three encores," Lilly went on. "Technically, she doesn't start hogging the spotlight until she's sung half a dozen."

"Hey! I was working hard out there," Miley protested, getting to her feet. She picked up a turkey sandwich and took a big bite before flopping back down in her chair. "I'm so tired, I can hardly move. Tomorrow I'm going to sleep in until noon at least!" She closed her eyes and smiled blissfully at the thought. "I can't wait to just kick back, chill out, and relax!"

"Whoa, bud, hold on a minute." Robby Ray Stewart, Miley's dad, had entered the room just in time to hear her last words.

Like Lilly, Mr. Stewart was in disguise. When he was acting as Hannah Montana's manager, he wore a fake mustache and a fedora. Right now, he was in full manager mode. "It's going to be another week before there's any kicking, chilling, or relaxing for you."

Miley's eyes popped open. "Manager, say what?" she asked.

"Remember, you have a photo shoot tomorrow," he said.

"I do?" Miley frowned as her daydream evaporated. "When?"

"Seven a.m.," her dad said. "On the dot."

"Seven in the morning!" Jackson chortled. "Man, that's like . . . dawn! And on a Saturday, too!" He shook his head, pretending to be sad. "Well, as *Entertainment Insider* always says, the life of a celebrity is very hard. How right they are."

Miley ignored him. "When did I agree to that?" she asked her dad.

"The same time you signed on for the radio press tour," he said. "You're doing eight radio interviews on Sunday, back to back."

"Eight!" Oliver looked impressed. "You'll be talking for hours. You could lose your voice!"

"That would be a bummer, wouldn't it?" Jackson put in gleefully. "If Hannah Montana—" His eyes widened with mock alarm as his voice dropped to a frantic whisper, "—*couldn't sing.*"

"Daddy!" Miley protested.

"Jackson, stop it," Mr. Stewart warned. "Miley's not going to lose her voice . . ."

Miley made a *so there* face at Jackson.

"'Cause she's got to sing at that hospital benefit on Monday night," her father went on. He pulled out his PDA and began scrolling through the calendar. "Then Tuesday is the charity softball game. Then we fly to Texas on Wednesday for the Lone Star Rodeo—"

Before he could go on, there was a knock on the door. An assistant poked her head inside. "Excuse me," he said. "Miss Montana's limo has arrived."

Oliver sighed happily. "No matter how many times I hear that," he said to Lilly, "it still sends a chill down my spine."

"I know!" Lilly said. "It's like in fairy tales when someone says, 'your carriage awaits,' only better."

"Yeah." Oliver nodded. "Carriages don't have moon roofs."

As they walked outside to the car, Miley's dad pulled her aside. "Hey, bud, are you okay?" he asked. "It's too late to cancel this week's schedule, but there's still time to bow out of the Texas concert. We can tell people you need your rest; they'll understand. . . ."

Lilly and Oliver exchanged pained looks. Mr. Stewart had invited them to go with Miley to the rodeo for a little vacation; he had even paid for their plane tickets. Not that they wouldn't be supportive if Miley was really too tired to go, but . . .

They didn't need to worry.

"Oh, no!" Miley said, opening her eyes wide in an attempt to look alert and energetic. "I *love* playing at the Lone Star Rodeo! And with Lilly and Oliver along for the ride, it'll feel more like a vacation than work."

"We did schedule some downtime for you," Mr. Stewart said. "I just want you to be sure you can handle it, that's all."

"I'm sure," Miley said. She settled into the leather seat, leaned her head back, and closed her eyes. "As soon as I get some sleep, I'll be rarin' to go. I promise."

Chapter Two

Talk slowly, think quickly.

—Traditional cowboy saying

Tuesday evening, after a four-hour photo shoot, a two-hour meeting with her publicist to discuss the radio interviews she had done, and a long session going over some new dance moves with her choreographer, Miley was even more exhausted than before.

She could have fallen into bed and slept through dinner, but Lilly and Oliver were coming over to eat. They had to finalize plans for meeting the next day to head to the airport and fly to Austin, Texas. So Miley wandered, yawning, onto the deck of the Stewart home and began setting the table with paper plates and napkins. The ocean was blue and gold in the setting sun, and even though it was late February, the evening was warm with just a hint of coolness.

There was also a delicious, tangy smell in the air that made Miley's stomach rumble with hunger and reminded her that it had now been five hours since the sandwich and mineral water she had gulped down for lunch.

She hurried to the end of the deck, where her father had set up his grill.

"Yum! Barbecue!" Miley's mouth started watering when she saw her father carefully turn over a piece of chicken he was cooking on the grill.

"I thought you deserved a little something special for working so hard," her dad said. "And Ol' Bessie hasn't been fired up for more than a month! She was feeling neglected."

Miley rolled her eyes, but only a little. She didn't want to put her dad in a bad mood. He always claimed he couldn't get his barbecue sauce right if he was in a "negative emotional state."

"Dad, you know that you're probably the only person in the world who names his barbecue grill, don't you?" she said.

"Yes, I do," he responded and added loftily, "And the world is poorer because of that sad fact."

Miley was still giggling at that when Lilly bounded up the stairs and onto the deck. "Hey, everybody! What's for dinner? I've been skateboarding all day, and I'm starving."

"Glad to hear it, Lilly," Miley's dad said. "Because I'm trying out a new and improved version of my already award-winning barbecue sauce, thanks to ol' Bessie." He fondly patted the grill, which he'd insisted on bringing from Tennessee when the family had relocated to California. It was weather-beaten after years of outdoor use; one leg was crooked from the time Jackson had run into it with the lawn mower; and it was black with age. But Robby

Stewart insisted that the grill was the secret behind his eleven consecutive blue ribbons in the annual mid-Tennessee barbecue cook-off.

"Yeah," he added, "Bessie's a real champ. And she's raring to get back into action."

Miley and Lilly exchanged a meaningful glance.

"Mr. Stewart," Lilly said, "you do know that grills don't have feelings, don't you?"

Before he had a chance to answer, a voice called out, "What's that you're saying, Lilly? Girls don't have feelings?"

Lilly groaned and dropped her head on the table as Jackson climbed up the stairs from the beach, followed closely by Oliver. Both boys' hair was sticking up in salty little spikes after an afternoon at the beach. Jackson turned to Oliver. "What did I tell you? I always suspected that girls just *pretended* to have all kinds of deep emotions in order to get us to do what they want! And now my darkest suspicions have been confirmed."

Oliver chuckled at Jackson's wit, then caught sight of Miley glaring at him. Instantly, he wiped the smile off his face. "Actually, Jackson, girls do have feelings," he said solemnly. "Very serious, important, tender feelings that we should always strive to keep from hurting."

"Nice try, man," Jackson snickered. He tossed Oliver a soda. "But you don't have to *completely* lose your dignity, you know. Dad's already bought your plane ticket."

Oliver popped open the soda can and nodded to Mr. Stewart. "Thank you again," he said, raising the can in a toast before taking a sip. "I am really looking forward to this culturally enriching experience."

Mr. Stewart's eyebrows shot up. "Say that again, Oliver? In words a good ol' boy like me can understand?"

"That's how my mom convinced my dad that I should go," Oliver explained, spearing a pickle from a jar on the table. "She said that it would be good for me to see how people live in a different part of the country. She said that it would broaden my horizons. And she said that it would give her a chance to redecorate my bedroom without having to wallpaper around me." He frowned. "I just hope I don't come home to find out that she's turned it into her crafts room."

Oliver bit into the pickle and winced at its sourness.

"Even if she does, it will be worth it," Miley promised. "The rodeo is so much fun! I can't wait to show you guys around." She started dancing around the deck. "I'm going to take you to the exhibits where kids show the pigs and chickens and cows they've been raising—"

"Come again?" Oliver looked dubious. "We're going on vacation to look at pigs?"

"You'll love it," Miley promised. "And we'll get to ride horses—"

"Um, yeah, about the horse thing," Lilly

interjected. "I'm not so sure that's really me, if you know what I mean."

"What are you talking about, Lilly?" Mr. Stewart asked, squinting at her through a sudden billow of grill smoke. "You're a total tomboy! I would have thought you couldn't wait to go for a gallop."

Lilly turned pale as Oliver's eyes grew wide. "A gallop?" Lilly echoed faintly. "Doesn't that mean going really, really fast?"

"Oh, don't worry you two," Miley answered. "Riding a horse is as easy as falling off a log. Trust me."

"The key word there is 'falling,'" Oliver pointed out. "Face it, Miley, I'm more of a twenty-first-century kind of guy. The internal combustion engine, that's the way I roll."

"You'll be fine," Miley said. "Trust me. We are going to have so much fun."

"Of course we will!" Lilly said brightly. After all, the three of them *had* been looking forward to this group vacation for months.

Surely they would find many, many things to do while they were in Texas. And if it just so happened that they ran out of time before they got around to riding horses . . . well, Lilly wouldn't be disappointed. "It's going to be such a cool trip," she said out loud. That reminded Lilly of what her mother had said before she left the house. She added quickly, "Thanks again for inviting us along, Mr. Stewart."

"My pleasure, Lilly," he said. "Besides, you kids are around here so much, sometimes I forget you aren't mine."

"Yeah, explain to me again how Miley gets to take *two* of her friends and I don't get to take any?" Jackson asked grumpily.

"I told you you could invite a friend," Mr. Stewart said. He flipped over a piece of chicken. "It's just too bad Thor had to back out, that's all."

Miley danced over to Jackson and patted him on the head. "Don't be sad, Jackson," she said sweetly. "Thor's just really, really busy, doing really, really important things." Then Miley coughed into her hand as she muttered, "Cheese."

Lilly snickered.

Her brother turned and glared at both of them. "It just so happens that being a judge at Minnoka, Minnesota's annual Cream Cheese Festival is a *very* big deal," he said. "And all my other *really* cool friends had better things to do than go look at cows in the middle of nowhere." He tossed a handful of chips into his mouth and grabbed a paper plate. "As a matter of fact, *I* have better things to be doing, too. I could be spending spring break in Malibu, soaking up the California sun and meeting cute California girls, but nooooo."

"Maybe we'll meet cute cowgirls instead," Oliver suggested.

"Yee-haw," Jackson said unenthusiastically. He scooped a helping of potato salad onto his plate and morosely took a bite. "Like I want to spend time with a girl who uses 'rodeo' as a verb."

"I would have thought you'd love to go to Texas," Lilly said. "I mean, you *are* from the South. Don't you want to return to your roots?"

"My roots have been transplanted," Jackson said firmly. "To the rich, nourishing soil of Malibu, California. And I don't want to pull them up again just to go to some stupid rodeo."

"Well, you'd better start digging yourself up and acting a little more excited," his father said. "Because here's the thing . . ." He stopped to turn over a piece of chicken.

Jackson eyed him suspiciously. "Here's what thing?"

"Well, you and Oliver and Lilly are all going to be hanging out with Hannah Montana for several days," Mr. Stewart said. "And we have to protect Miley's secret identity as Hannah Montana. So I had to come up with a reason for you two boys to be tagging along."

"Hey, I have an idea!" Oliver's face lit up. "We could pretend to be Miley's bodyguards! We could wear cool sunglasses like those Secret Service guys who guard the president! And we could get earpieces and microphones that would let us talk to each other—"

"Not a bad idea," Mr. Stewart said. "But I've already figured out something a little more . . . creative."

"Like what?" Jackson asked, his suspicions growing.

His dad grinned.

"Come on, tell me." Jackson was officially starting to panic.

His dad started to chuckle.

"Please! If it's bad news, just give it to me straight!" Jackson cried. "I don't care what it is. It's knowing that something bad is coming but not knowing what that bad thing *is* that's horrible. It's torture. . . ."

Finally, Mr. Stewart took pity on his son.

"Okay, here's your cover story," he said. "You won a contest—"

"A contest?" Jackson calmed down a little. That didn't sound too bad. . . .

"Yep. You wrote an essay, and your prize is a trip for you and a friend—that's you, Oliver—to the Lone Star Rodeo with none other than pop sensation Hannah Montana! The trip will end with special box seats at her sold-out concert."

"Cool!" Oliver held up his right hand to high-five Jackson. "Way to go, Jackson!"

Jackson raised his hand, not for a high five, but to signal caution. "Whoa. Wait a minute." He narrowed his eyes at his dad. "You wouldn't be grinning like that if you didn't have a surprise up your sleeve."

Mr. Stewart tried to look innocent and failed. "Oh, I guess I did forget one little thing," he said, pulling his digital camera out of his pocket. "The title of your essay?"

Jackson braced himself. "Yeah . . ."

"It was called 'Why I'm Hannah Montana's Number One Fan,'" his dad said.

"What?!" Jackson screeched.

Mr. Stewart held up the camera and took a few quick shots of Jackson's anguished face, then glanced at the screen. "Oh, yeah," he chuckled. "That's definitely gotta go on this year's Christmas card."

He held the camera out so that Miley and Lilly could take a look. They began laughing so hard that they both snorted soda through their noses.

Mr. Stewart took a picture of that, too.

"Hey!" Lilly protested.

"I knew I wouldn't regret paying extra for the stop-motion feature," he said.

"Dad!" Jackson cried. He had suffered many injustices in his life, but this one topped them all. He barely knew where to start his protest. Finally, he just said, "This is totally unfair!"

"Really? I thought it was kind of clever,"

Mr. Stewart said. "Anyway, I know *I'll* be entertained watching you fall all over your sister for a week."

Miley snickered. "You better start practicing, Jackson," she said. "I want to hear the words 'super,' 'talented,' 'sensational,' and 'star' at least once an hour." She waved one hand airily. "Any combination is fine."

"Okay." Jackson thought for a minute, then said, "Hannah Montana is a SUPER annoying STAR whose TALENT will make everyone around her go insane because they can't get her SENSATIONAL songs out of their heads!"

Miley smiled at him. "I like it!"

"Hey, maybe we can figure out a way to use the words 'incredible,' 'fantastic,' and 'amazing,' too," Oliver suggested earnestly to Jackson. "We could work on it during the plane ride."

"Thanks, bro," Jackson snapped. "Glad to see you have my back."

"What?" Oliver asked, confused by the other boy's bitter tone.

"Now that's what I like to see," Mr. Stewart said, pointing his spatula at Oliver. "In fact, that's a FAN-tastic attitude, Oliver."

Oliver beamed proudly as everyone else groaned at Mr. Stewart's pun.

"Speaking of fans," Lilly said, "you know that Lola is not just Hannah's fan but a true friend. . . ."

"I know, I know." Miley rolled her eyes. "I've already told you a million times, I'll be sure to introduce you to Joshua McAdams."

Lilly jumped up and hugged Miley, squealing with delight.

"Hey!" Miley rubbed the ear Lilly had just squealed into. "I told you, stop doing that!"

"What's the big deal about Joshua McAdams?" Oliver asked.

"*This* is the big deal!" Lilly flapped a brochure for the Lone Star Rodeo in Oliver's face. She had read it so many times over the last month that it was now creased and wrinkled.

"He's so cute! And he's going to perform in concert with Hannah Montana!" She stopped waving the brochure long enough to stare at his picture. "I just love his song, 'Let Your Heart Go.' And you know how, in the video, he dances across the lawn with the sprinklers going? *Super* cool."

"Oh, yeah, it's well done," Miley said in a professional tone. She liked Joshua's music, but she didn't get all starry-eyed over him the way Lilly did. Still, it would be nice to meet someone her own age who was also in the music business and had to deal with the same kind of pressures. . . .

"I think we might have a lot in common," she finished.

"Oh, yes, you do," Lilly said earnestly. "*You* have a very good friend named Lilly and Joshua McAdams would be delighted to *meet* your very good friend Lilly. See? You and

Joshua will have an immediate bond, thanks to me!"

Miley laughed. "Yeah, right," she said. "Thanks for pointing that out."

"I can't believe I'm going to meet him!" Lilly shrieked. "The biggest pop star in the universe!"

"Excuse me, Lilly," Oliver said. "I believe that *Hannah Montana* is the biggest pop star in the universe."

Miley smiled. "Aw, thanks, Oli—"

But Oliver had already turned toward Mr. Stewart. "How was that? Did I sound like her number one fan?"

"You bet." Mr. Stewart gave him a thumbs up, then nodded meaningfully at his son. "You may want to take a few acting lessons from Oliver here."

Oliver smiled smugly at Jackson.

"Now, is everybody ready to eat?" Mr. Stewart asked, piling one platter high with barbecued chicken and another with burgers.

Everyone nodded and they sat down and began serving themselves. Despite Jackson's disgruntlement over being cast as Hannah's fan, Miley's disappointment that she was going to have Jackson as a chaperone, and Lilly's secret fear that she was not going to get along well with horses, the first bite of barbecue made everyone momentarily happy.

Mr. Stewart closed his eyes for a moment, a blissful expression on his face as he chewed. "Now that's good barbecue."

"It is *excellent* barbecue," Oliver added. "In fact, I'd say it's excellent enough to be served to Hannah Montana herself!"

As everyone good-naturedly booed him, they felt a surge of excitement. Tomorrow they would all be getting on a plane and heading off for another adventure . . . together.

Chapter Three

Never approach a bull from the front, a horse from the rear, or a fool from any direction.
                        —Traditional cowboy saying

"Well, hello, little lady!" A large man wearing a blue suit, a black string tie, and a cowboy hat strode across the hotel lobby to where Hannah Montana, Lola Luftnagle, Oliver, Jackson, and Hannah's manager were standing in the middle of a sea of luggage. He was holding out his hand for the pop star to shake. "I'm Jim Bob Cooper, the president of the Lone Star Rodeo Association, and I'm just pleased as punch to meet you! I hope y'all had a good trip."

"Easy as pie," Miley said, smiling her brightest smile. She was wearing her long blond wig, full makeup, and a sequined red jacket, embroidered jeans, and gold sandals. She felt ridiculously overdressed for one o'clock in the afternoon, but she knew she had to be in full Hannah Montana mode from the moment she stepped off the plane in Texas. "Thank you for setting everything up for us, Mr. Cooper."

"Now, darlin', I don't want to hear any of that 'Mr. Cooper' business," he said with a smile. "Everybody just calls me Jim Bob."

"Well, thank you, Jim Bob." Miley gestured toward Lilly and her father. "This is my dear friend, Lola Luftnagle, and my manager."

"Howdy," Jim Bob turned toward Jackson and Oliver and grinned even more broadly. "And these two must be the lucky young fellas who won the contest!"

"Yes, sir!" Oliver said brightly. "Actually, Jackson wrote the winning essay. But I'm a big Hannah Montana fan, too. That's why it makes total sense that we're both here with her on this trip. No one should even think twice about our presence. There shouldn't be the slightest question in anyone's mind about why we're tagging along with an internationally famous pop star—"

"Um, yeah, thanks, Oliver." Mr. Stewart stepped in hastily. He whispered to Jim Bob, "The kid's a little excited. Plus, he had a few too many sodas on the plane."

"Caffeine can take some people that way," Jim Bob said, nodding. He turned to Jackson. "Now, son, you seem more on the shy side."

Behind his back, Miley and Lilly rolled their eyes at each other. Shy? Jackson?

But Jim Bob was determined to coax Jackson out of his "shell." "I know it's a little intimidating for you, not being from a show-biz background and all," he said. "But I'd sure like to hear what you wrote in that winning essay. It must have been real special for you to beat out thousands of other contestants."

"Yes, I'd like to hear that, too," Miley said sweetly. Her father gave her a warning look, and she added quickly, "I mean, I read the essay, of course, when I did the final judging, but it's been a long time. I don't remember all the points."

Everyone looked at Jackson.

Jackson looked back at the circle of expectant faces. There was no way out. Silently vowing to pay Miley back if it took him years and years and years, even until he was an old man of forty, he said, "Well, I like her songs, you know, because, um . . ."

His voice trailed off. Miley leaned toward him and smiled. "*What* do you like about them?" she asked with wide-eyed wonder. "I'd just *love* to know!"

He glared at her. "They have a lot of pep," he said through gritted teeth. "And, er, harmony. And other good musical stuff like that."

Lilly stifled a giggle. "What about her personality?" she asked, doing her best to keep a straight face. "Isn't there some little thing she does that you find particularly endearing?"

"No," Jackson snapped. Jim Bob looked surprised. His father narrowed his eyes in a menacing way, so Jackson quickly added, "That is, I think that *everything* Hannah does is endearing!"

Next to him, Oliver nodded in approval. He knew Jackson was a fast talker but *that* was impressive! And he had even sounded kind of . . . sweet.

Then Oliver saw a slight grin appear on Jackson's face. He braced himself. He knew that grin all too well. It was the little grin that said Jackson had just thought of a really excellent way to tease his sister.

"Like the way she picks her teeth after she's had corn on the cob," Jackson went on cheerfully. "Now, a lot of girls in her position would be too snooty to do that, but not

Hannah! She's a country girl at heart, and she's going to stay real! And then there's the way soda makes her burp in a completely charming way. Oh, and I almost forgot—"

"Okay, okay," Mr. Stewart said, quickly moving in between Jackson and Miley, who looked as if she was about to forget she was Hannah Montana and wrestle her brother to the ground—as if they were in their own living room. "We get the point."

"Well, son," Jim Bob said, grinning. "I gotta say, you sure do sound like a huge fan. And you are going to be mighty busy, because we have a jam-packed schedule for Hannah," he added.

As Jim Bob went in search of a bellboy to take their luggage to their rooms, Miley's attention was caught by a commotion near the registration desk. A knot of concerned people huddled around someone who was obviously displeased. She heard that person say, "I don't care if the penthouse suite is already occupied!

That's the room I told my assistant to book, and that's the room I want."

"I'm sorry, sir," the hotel manager said in a harassed voice. "We'll certainly find a way to make you happy. Perhaps another luxury suite and a room-service dinner, on the house?"

Just then, the crowd moved slightly, and Miley saw that the customer who was raising such a fuss was none other than Joshua McAdams. He looked just the way he did in his "Let Your Heart Go" video—or almost. He still had that perfectly cut blond hair and those electric blue eyes, but he wasn't smiling, so his charming dimple had vanished. His expression was peevish instead of soulful. And his voice, usually so smooth, was now as cranky as a sleepy toddler's.

Miley's eyes slid sideways to see if Lilly had noticed that her pop-star crush was on the premises . . . and throwing a major tantrum.

Lilly most certainly had. She looked over at Miley, her expression shocked. "Did you hear that?" she whispered. "I had no idea Joshua McAdams was such a jerk!"

"Neither did I," Miley whispered back. "I guess music videos don't always tell the truth, huh?"

Before they could discuss this further, Jim Bob came back, a bellboy in tow. "All right, we're good to go," he said, ushering them into the elevator, then squinting at his clipboard as the doors closed. "I'll give you a copy of your itinerary, but here are the highlights. There's your big concert on the last night of the rodeo, of course. Already sold out, by the way. Between now and then, we've scheduled a tour of the booths in our shopping area, just in case you want to pick up a cowboy hat for your stay in Texas."

"Cool," Miley said. "I can always use another cowboy hat."

Jackson rolled his eyes. He'd *never* wear a hat that made him look like someone who had gotten lost on his way to a costume party!

There was a ding as they arrived on the

thirtieth floor. Jim Bob led them down the hallway to their rooms, still reading out loud from his clipboard. "We also have a walk-through at the animal and agricultural booths, with a photo op or two," he said. "We've got an impressive bunch of farm animals this year, I tell you what. There's a red bantam that has prizewinner written all over her."

"I can't wait to see that," Miley said in the polite tone Hannah would use.

Jackson wasn't nearly as polite. They were going to spend hours looking at cows and chickens? He practically yawned but cheered himself up with the thought that things couldn't possibly get worse. . . .

"Then we'll make sure you get a chance to attend some of the other fantastic events we put on here at the rodeo," Jim Bob said. "There's the pig race and the calf scramble. And, of course, every night, there's bull riding, bronco busting, and barrel racing."

Pig races? Calf scrambles?

Okay. I was wrong, Jackson thought. Things just got worse.

But Jim Bob wasn't done talking.

"And we will be driving you out to do a meet-and-greet with the trail ride," he added. "That's a bunch of people who saddle up their horses, outfit some real old-fashioned covered wagons, and ride to the rodeo. Some of them travel hundreds of miles to get here."

"That's so cool!" Miley said, her eyes sparkling. She turned to Lilly. "Doesn't that sound like fun, Lil—I mean, Lola?"

"Oh. Yeah. Superfun," Lilly said rather unenthusiastically.

Jackson caught her eye and shook his head sadly. He knew that, in this case at least, he and Lilly were totally on the same page. Who would choose to spend days riding a horse when they could drive a car? Not only were cars faster, but they had air conditioning, and they didn't step on your foot, kind of accidentally on purpose, the way horses did.

The picture of dejection, Jackson's shoulders slumped, and he began dragging his feet as they walked down the hall.

This trip was turning into a real bust. Nothing but cows and horses and photo ops with chickens. When he thought about what he would be doing at this very minute if he were back in Malibu—when he thought about the surf and the sand and the girls in bathing suits—Jackson wanted to cry. He wasn't even going to have a room to himself, the way he did at home! He was going to have to share with Oliver!

Just as Jackson started a mental countdown of how many days he had to suffer through before getting back to his real life, Jim Bob stopped in front of a door.

"Let's see," Jim Bob said, double-checking his list. "Hannah, we reserved the presidential suite for you, but it's not quite ready. Why don't we go into suite 3012—that's got a room for Jackson and Oliver and another room for

Mr. Stewart—and y'all can relax a little bit." He flung the door open and gestured for everyone to enter. "I hope you'll feel right at home."

Jackson only took four steps past the door before he stopped dead. As he gazed around the room, he halfway expected to hear a chorus of angelic voices. It was a suite, with two bedrooms and a living room with a panoramic view . . . well, okay, it was a panoramic view of the parking lot, but still. And there was a forty-two-inch plasma screen TV! With a state-of-the-art video game system! And a welcome basket filled with snacks and sodas! And—he ran over to open the bathroom door—a jacuzzi!

"Yeah," he said as offhandedly as he could, given that his mind was filled with thoughts of room service and hours spent battling Oliver in *Red Planet Conquest IV*. "I guess we can make this work."

Jim Bob nodded. Happy the boys were

satisfied, he turned back to Miley. "And, of course, you'll be one of our celebrity judges at the Lone Star Rodeo beauty pageant."

"Tough job, Hannah," Jackson said, grinning. He stretched out on the sofa and crossed his arms behind his head.

How had he missed the fact that Miley was going to be surrounded by a bunch of beauty pageant contestants? An even happier thought struck him. Those beauty pageant contestants would probably be very interested in getting to know the guy who was *this close* with one of the judges. . . .

This trip was suddenly looking up—way up in fact.

"I'm sure I can handle it," Miley said, raising one eyebrow in a way that told him she knew *exactly* what he was thinking. And that she didn't like it one bit.

Jim Bob turned to Miley and Lilly. "I'll take you girls up to the presidential suite and leave you fellas to get settled. Then I'll see you tomorrow morning, bright and early, to take you to the trail ride. You kids have a good time this afternoon."

"Oh, we will," Jackson replied, snickering a bit as Jim Bob left. Maybe this gig could turn out to be more fun than he had expected! After all, he got to torture his sister at every turn. Who could ask for a better vacation than that?

Chapter Four

Lettin' the cat outta the bag is a whole lot easier than puttin' it back.

—Traditional cowboy saying

"Come on, let's check out the midway!" Miley said excitedly. "Or maybe we should swing by the pie-judging booth? Oh, wait, that might make us too hungry. . . . How about the vegetable-judging booth? One time I saw a fifty-pound squash at the county fair back home! What do you think, Lilly?"

But Lilly was too busy turning her head this way and that, trying to take in all the sights and sounds of the fairgrounds, to answer. After they had unpacked their suitcases in the penthouse—which was even bigger than Jackson's and her dad's suite, with a much better view—Miley and Lilly had quickly changed their clothes, stowed their wigs, and then snuck down the back stairs so that no one would see two ordinary teenagers leaving Hannah Montana's suite.

Giggling, they raced through the lobby and hopped on a bus that took them to the rodeo fairgrounds. As they walked through the midway, filled with the smell of popcorn and cotton candy, Lilly's head swiveled back and forth.

"I've never seen so many cowboy hats in my life," Lilly said as she stared at the crowd of people wandering from one exhibit to the next.

"I know!" Miley said. "Isn't it great?"

But Lilly wasn't listening. She was staring at a shed covered by a tin roof. There was a sign outside that read, PIG RACES EVERY HOUR! On the sign was a painting of a pig racing around a track, a number on its back and a determined expression on its face. "I've heard of horse races and dog races, but . . . pig races?"

"Oh, yeah, that's so cute!" Miley said enthusiastically. "The pigs race for cookies! And there's a special pig who swims in a little pool—"

But they had strolled on toward another outdoor shed that advertised: MUTTON BUSTIN' CONTEST!

"Mutton bustin'?" Lilly asked, sounding as if she had landed on an alien planet instead of in Texas.

"Oh, we've got to watch that." Miley smiled. She was enjoying the experience of showing her friend around and explaining this world to her. It was a definite role reversal. Back in Malibu, she always felt like Lilly was doing the explaining. "It's like a little kids' version of bronco busting, except they ride sheep instead of horses. And, of course, the sheep don't buck them off, they just run around like mad."

Lilly's eyebrows were raised practically to her hairline. "They ride sheep?!"

"It's cool," Miley reassured her. "We'll come back in a couple of hours and watch. But first, it's time to do some shopping!"

Lilly nodded vigorously. Pig races and sheep riding were foreign concepts to her, but *shopping* . . . that was a language she understood.

Miley stopped at a booth selling cowboy hats and picked up a straw one that was tinted lavender, plopping it on Lilly's head. "That looks fantastic on you! Why don't you get it?"

Lilly peered doubtfully at her reflection in the booth's mirror. "I don't know," she said. "I'm not sure a cowboy hat is really . . . me. I'm more of a California girl—"

"Who happens to be in Texas now!" Miley said breezily. She pulled out her wallet. "I'm getting it for you as a souvenir of our trip. You look too great to pass it up."

"Well, thanks," Lilly said.

"In fact—" Miley picked up a red version of Lilly's hat and tried it on. "What do you think? Definite, possibility, or pass?"

This was their shopping shorthand: "definite" meant "buy it now or you'll regret it for the rest of your life"; "possibility" meant "wait and see if you find something you like better"; and "pass" meant "you'll wear it once, then shove it to the back of the closet."

When Miley and Lilly hit the mall back home, they always consulted each other before buying anything, and they had made a pact to always tell the unvarnished truth. It was a serious pact, so Lilly turned away from the mirror and gave Miley a long, considered look before rendering her decision.

Finally, she nodded. "That's a definite. You look like you were born to wear a cowboy hat."

"I think I kind of was!" Miley laughed as she paid for the hats. "I mean, growing up on a farm, we always had some livestock around the place. Chickens, goats, pigs . . . oh, and did I ever tell you about Doc?"

"Doc? The horse you learned to ride on? The one who was black with a white star on his forehead, who ran like the wind and jumped the tallest fences with ease? The horse that all other horses must be measured against in the future?" Lilly asked. "That horse?"

"Okay, okay, I guess I have told you a little bit about him," Miley said. She sighed wistfully. "I still miss Doc. Did I ever tell you about the time he was running around the pasture and I was trying to rope him and—"

"You missed and fell face-first into a mud puddle? But you got right back up and managed to lasso him? And ever since that day, the two of you were the best of friends?" Lilly finished. "Yeah. You told me."

"Okay, okay, maybe I do go on about Doc a little bit," Miley admitted.

"A little bit? We'd known each other for

months before I realized he wasn't your old boyfriend from Tennessee!" Lilly said.

Giggling, they walked a few yards down the aisle, peering around the crowds of shoppers to see what was for sale in each booth. Suddenly, Miley stopped dead and grabbed Lilly's arm.

"Oh, look at those necklaces," she said. "They're gorgeous, aren't they? And I was just thinking the other day that a turquoise necklace would look great with the costume I'm wearing for my last song!"

"Sounds like fate to me," Lilly said agreeably. She drifted over to take a look, even though she didn't care much for jewelry.

Miley walked over and picked up a turquoise pendant on a silver chain. The turquoise was carved in the shape of a bucking bronco. "This one would be perfect—"

"Excuse me, hon," a voice interrupted. It was a sweet, honeyed voice, but it had a dash of vinegar. "Can I help you?"

A thin, blond woman with a lacquered pageboy hairdo smiled thinly, one overplucked eyebrow raised haughtily. She nodded toward the necklace in Miley's hand.

"Oh, no, I was just looking," Miley said.

The woman reached out and gently but firmly took the necklace away from her. "I'm afraid my items might be a little too . . . high-end for a teenager's budget, darlin'. But I do appreciate your interest."

Miley flushed with embarrassment. Before she could stop herself, she said, "Actually, I was just thinking I might want to buy that."

"But we have somewhere else we should be," Lilly said quickly. She glanced at her watch and pretended to jump with surprise. "And we're already so, so late! Come on, *Miley*."

She grabbed Miley's shoulders, swung her around, and marched her over to the exhibit hall doors. "Remember, you're not Hannah Montana," she hissed. "At least, not right now."

"I know I'm not!" Miley turned to glare at

the woman, who was carefully putting the necklace back on a jewelry stand. "She doesn't know that! For all she knows, I'm a princess from a small but very wealthy country who was ready to buy every necklace in her booth!"

Lilly looked her up and down, and grinned.

"What?" Miley asked.

"A princess?" Lilly repeated. "With that big nacho-cheese stain on your shirt?"

Miley looked down. "Oh, sweet niblets."

Thirty minutes later, Miley and Lilly had shared a supersized tub of popcorn, staggered along the sloping floors of the funhouse, and tried their hand at half a dozen midway games. Lilly was carrying a huge, stuffed purple teddy bear after a successful session at ring toss, whereas Miley had won only a small plastic keychain at the air-rifle booth—and that was after using up all her tickets to take five turns in a row.

"I still think that game was rigged," she

said, twirling the keychain around one finger.

"Or, and this is just for argument's sake, you have absolutely no hand-eye coordination," Lilly snickered. Miley pretended to glare at her, and Lilly shrugged. "Just a theory," Lilly said cheerfully. Then her nose wrinkled, and her smile disappeared. "Ooh! What's that smell?"

Miley sniffed the air. Her face brightened. "We must be near the hall where the 4-H kids exhibit their animals!"

"Oh, so dat's whad dat smell is," Lilly said, holding her nose. Too late, she remembered Jackson's ominous warnings about manure.

"Come on, Lilly, you'll love this," Miley promised. "And after ten minutes, you won't notice the smell at all."

It took more than ten minutes, but Lilly had to admit that Miley was right. It was pretty cool to get up close and personal with a rooster, an animal she'd never seen outside the pages of a picture book. The cow-milking demonstration was an eye opener, too; Lilly silently promised herself that she'd drink her daily glass of milk with more respect in the future. And all the newborn animals—some of them, like the little calves that had been born just an hour ago and were still struggling to get to their feet—were completely adorable.

They were walking down the sawdust-covered aisle toward the farm-animal exhibits when they saw a boy about their own age standing in front of a huge spotted pig in a pen. The boy was wearing jeans, a button-down plaid shirt, and a cowboy hat, but what caught their attention—and the attention of many people walking by—was that he was practicing rope tricks. The boy would send his lariat looping out across the floor in lazy circles, then pull it back in. Every once in a while, he would manage to rope the foot of a passing girl, who would giggle and stop to chat for a spell. Miley could see why, too. He had dark eyes, a sprinkling of freckles on his nose, and his hair (what she could see of it under the hat) was dark brown.

"He's kinda cute," Miley whispered.

"You think any guy in a cowboy hat is cute," Lilly countered.

"That's not true!" Miley said automatically. Then she stopped and thought for a second. "Oh, wait," she giggled. "You're right, I do."

"Uh-huh." Lilly looked smug. "Face it, no one knows you like I do."

Miley snuck another quick peek at the boy in the cowboy hat. Although he seemed focused on what he was doing, Miley could tell that he was aware of the interested and admiring glances from people who were passing by. Then three girls walked down the aisle, and Miley saw him grin slightly to himself.

All three girls were pretty, but one was clearly a standout. She had long black hair, bright blue eyes, and a vivacious smile. She was chattering animatedly to her two companions, who seemed to be doing most of the listening. The girl wore a silver lamé halter top, black silk pants, and high-heeled black sandals, which Miley thought was a little over-the-top for a livestock show.

And a moment later, Miley also thought the outfit was rather impractical, because just then the boy twirled his rope one more time and caught the girl's foot by its strappy sandal.

"Hey!" she yelled with irritation as she tripped and fell forward.

The boy jumped and caught her in his arms, almost as if he'd practiced it.

"Sorry about that, m'am," he said, leaning down to release her foot. "I guess my lasso just got away from me." He stood up and tipped his hat back with one finger. "'Course, sometimes when I rope something by mistake, it turns out to be a lucky accident."

"Really." The girl tossed her hair back over her shoulder and stared down her nose at him. She wasn't smiling. "Is that you?"

She pointed at the black-and-white photo on the back of the pigpen. It showed the boy standing proudly next to the spotted pig, holding a blue ribbon in the air.

"Um, yeah." He blushed, but raised his chin proudly. "And that's Sweet Pea. He was the runt of the litter, but I raised him until he got fat and sassy."

She rolled her eyes. "That's sooo impressive," she said insincerely.

"Wow," Lilly said. "I can't believe she's turning down a chance to flirt with him."

"Yeah . . ." Miley said, narrowing her eyes to view the girl more carefully. There was something about that jet-black hair that seemed strangely familiar, but she couldn't put a finger on what it was.

The boy's smile slipped a bit, but he didn't give up. "My name's Cash," he said. "Cash Garrity."

The girl raised one eyebrow. "My name's Ima," she said, a little too sweetly.

Cash looked relieved at this pleasant response. "Nice to meet you, Ima—" he began.

She cut him off. "As in, Ima outta here."

Miley frowned, both because the remark was so mean and because there was something about the sound of the girl's voice that rang a faint bell. . . .

"How rude!" Lilly exclaimed.

The girl spun on her heel and walked away from Cash, heading in Miley and Lilly's direction. After a few steps, she turned her head to say over her shoulder, "Just to be clear, I *might* date a cowboy. But I don't even talk to *pig farmers*."

As the girl stalked toward them, followed by her giggling friends, Miley saw her face, and suddenly everything clicked into place.

"Angela!" she said.

As the girl hesitated at the sound of her name, Lilly whispered, "Do you know her?"

"Yeah, from Tennessee," Miley said. She waved at Angela, a little uncertainly. The girl she remembered had been a grade ahead of her in school and really cool. The girl she remembered would never have been so rude to someone like Cash, who was now blushing and coiling his rope as quickly as he could. The girl she remembered would certainly have remembered her. . . .

But Angela was striding right past Miley, her nose in the air. Miley felt a little spurt of anger at being so obviously ignored. "Angela!" she called out more loudly. "Remember me? Miley Stewart? From Crowley Corners?"

For a split second, it seemed that Angela might still decide to pretend she hadn't heard, but her two friends had stopped automatically, so she did, too. She coolly appraised Miley, from the top of her head (too late, Miley wished she had done more than just pull her brown hair back into a rather messy ponytail) to the tips of her shoes (with sudden blazing clarity, Miley remembered the hole in the toe of her favorite sneakers), then returned to her face, which Angela examined with puzzled amusement. "Miley?" she repeated in a distant voice. "Mmm, no, I don't think—"

"Oh, come on!" Miley could feel her face getting red with both irritation and embarrassment. "We took baton twirling together in elementary school! You helped me learn how to do a figure eight, and I got you a cold cloth the time you missed that high catch and the baton thonked you right on your—"

"Yes, right, now I remember!" Angela said loudly. She turned toward her two friends and said, not so softly under her breath, "You know how it is once you start getting famous. Everyone from your past claims they were your best friend."

"Such a pain," one of the girls said.

"Part of the price of celebrity," the other one added wisely.

"You guys can go back to the hotel if you want," Angela said. "I'll catch up with you later."

"Cool," they said in unison. "See ya."

They flipped identical waves and walked off without a backward glance.

Angela turned her attention back to Miley. "So, Miley . . . um—"

"Stewart," Miley said evenly. "Does that jog your memory?"

"Oh, right." Angela snapped her fingers, as though she hadn't known all along. "Miley Stewart. I should have known we knew each other way back then, because you called me Angela."

"Right," Miley said. "Because that's your name."

"Now I go by my middle name," said the girl-formerly-known-as-Angela. "Peyton."

"Oh. Well. That's a good name, too," Miley said, slightly taken aback. "It sounds very . . . aristocratic."

Peyton thawed a tiny bit. "Exactly," she said. "That was the effect we wanted."

"We?"

"Team Peyton," she explained. "A few years ago, we—that is, my dad and I—decided that I should go on the beauty-pageant circuit. I was way behind the other girls, though, since I didn't start when I was three. So he hired a pageant coach and a costume consultant. Of course, I also have a hair-and-makeup stylist on retainer, and we stepped up my private voice and piano tutoring to three times a week."

"Huh," Miley said. "So your dad hired all those people just to help you . . . win beauty pageants?"

Peyton didn't seem to hear the note of doubt in Miley's voice. "Absolutely," she said. "Every month, Team Peyton gets together and has a meeting to go over strategy and tactics. A year ago, we mapped out all the major competitions that I should enter. Six months ago, I started working with a personal trainer at the gym so that I would be in totally awesome shape by the time the major fall pageants start. And then three months ago, we changed my name. After *that* I won my first state pageant and got to come here."

"That's great," Miley said politely. "It sounds like you've been working really hard."

"Of course!" Peyton said, wide-eyed. "After all, when you're in the beauty pageant big leagues, you have to have more than looks and talent and poise. My coach says you also have to have the three Ps: Perfect. Pageant. Presentation. *That's* what it takes to win."

Lilly nudged Miley hard, which Miley correctly interpreted as, *You're looking like an idiot right now.* Miley closed her mouth, which had been hanging open in utter amazement, and tried to gather her thoughts.

"Well, yeah, I guess it is," she managed to say. "I mean, if winning is the point."

Now it was Peyton's turn to look amazed. "Of course it is! How else am I supposed to escape from Tennessee?"

"What do you mean, 'escape'?" Miley asked. "I was just feeling so homesick for Tennessee!"

Peyton gave her an incredulous glance. "But I heard you moved to California," she said. "That's where all the movie stars live, isn't it? Why would you care about some little life in Tennessee?"

"Because, I don't know . . . because it feels like home," Miley said. Lame-o, she thought to herself. Can't you come up with something that doesn't sound like a cheesy greeting card?

Peyton tossed her head. "I may have started out there, but I know I'm destined for something bigger," she said. "I can't wait to leave small-town life behind, the sooner the better."

"Right," Miley said weakly. Her head was spinning a bit. After all, she had left small-town Tennessee life in order to follow her dreams. And she had worked just as hard as Angela— that is, Peyton—to make her dreams come true. And she also had support from people like her dad and her publicist and her costume designer. . . .

So why did she feel so uneasy about the change she saw in her old friend?

Before she could say anything else, an agitated man came rushing up to them. He looked slicker than Miley remembered—his brown hair had been styled, not just cut, and he was wearing a sharp suit and trendy glasses—but she still recognized Mr. Fredericks, Peyton's father.

"There you are, Peyton!" he said without even glancing at Miley or Lilly. "I've been looking everywhere for you! Shashanna has made some adjustments to your evening gown. You need to come back to the hotel right away for another fitting." His voice had an edge to it as he added, "Didn't you check your agenda today?"

"Sorry, Dad." Peyton looked crestfallen. "A couple of the girls in the pageant wanted to walk around a little bit. I guess I forgot."

He looked even more exasperated. "You forgot an important appointment *and* you were fraternizing with your competitors?" he said, his voice getting a little louder. "Where's your head these days, Peyton? You want to win, don't you?"

Miley thought she saw a shimmer of tears in Peyton's eyes. "Of course I do, Dad, you know that," Peyton said, her voice trembling.

"Because if you don't want to win, I don't know why we're going to all this trouble and spending all this money," her dad went on. "We could all be living a quiet, stress-free life back in Tennessee if all you're interested in is running around with your friends—"

"Excuse me, Mr. Fredericks." Miley decided it was time—past time, in fact—for her to step in. "I don't know if you remember me? Miley Stewart? I was one year behind Angela—"

"She's called Peyton now," he snapped. "Nice to see you again, Molly. Come on, Peyton. There's a reception tonight for all the pageant contestants and judges. Both Hannah Montana and Joshua McAdams will be there.

This is a golden opportunity to make a good impression, and I don't want you to waste it."

"Of course not, Dad," Peyton said. She flashed a faint version of her bright smile in Miley and Lilly's direction. "I probably won't run into you again, but it was nice seeing you." Then she trailed off after her father.

After she was gone, Lilly just looked at Miley. "Are you kidding? She used to be your friend?"

"I don't know what happened!" Miley said. "She used to be so cool and down-to-earth. I mean, she was friendly to everybody, even people like me who were younger than she was."

"Maybe we just ran into her evil twin," Lilly said, her eyes sparkling with delight at the idea. "You know, like in that movie we watched on that weird cable channel, the one where the evil twin joins forces with the mutants and—"

"Yeah, okay, I remember that movie and it was awesome, but this is real life," Miley said.

"And it's plain weird. How could she have changed so much?"

"Maybe aliens took over her body?" Lilly suggested as she started walking, steering Miley toward a booth that was selling cotton candy. "You know, like that other movie we saw, the one where the people all start acting like zombies and—"

"Right, another great movie with no bearing on our everyday existence," Miley said. She really couldn't wait until Lilly's horror-movie phase was over. "It's so strange. It's not like everyone who wants to get into show business has to leave their real self behind . . . right?"

But Lilly wasn't listening. "I don't know," she shrugged. "But Peyton would probably freak out if she knew she just blew off one of the judges."

"Yeah," Miley nodded. "It sure will be interesting to see her later at the pageant." She looked over her shoulder, but Peyton was long gone. "I mean, I'm supposed to be an impartial judge, but that'll be hard if she has an attitude like that."

"Don't worry so much." Lilly handed Miley a pink cotton candy, took a blue one for herself, and paid for both. "After all, you could totally keep her from winning if you wanted to."

"I wouldn't do that," Miley said automatically, but now it was her turn to be preoccupied. She couldn't believe how much different Angela— *Peyton*—was now. It bothered her in some way that she couldn't quite figure out. After all, everybody grew up, everybody changed, everybody had her own path to take. . . .

Before she could pursue that line of thought any further, Jackson and Oliver came rushing up to them, waving half-eaten corn dogs in the air.

"Hey, Miley! Lilly!" Oliver shouted. "You should try these corn dogs. They're awesome."

"I'm sure they are, but we don't need a preview," Lilly said in disgust.

He gave her a puzzled glance, still chewing. "What?"

She rolled her eyes. "You're talking with your mouth full, Oliver!"

He swallowed. "Oops, sorry."

"I may not be down with pigs and cows and bronco busting," Jackson said, "but the food here is great. Look!" He held up his left hand, which held several half-nibbled snacks. "They've got sausage on a stick! They've got cheesecake on a stick! They've got *everything* on a stick!"

"That's great, Jackson," Miley said. "At last you've found the place you fit in, a place that doesn't require certain basics of civilization, like cutlery."

"I know you didn't mean it that way," Jackson said, "but I'm taking that as a compliment."

Still laughing and teasing one another, the four drifted toward the door. As they walked out into the sunshine, Miley glanced over her shoulder again and saw the boy in the cowboy hat, who had gone back to spinning his rope across the floor.

She smiled to herself. Maybe Peyton wasn't interested in talking to someone who raised pigs, she thought. But Miley Stewart certainly was.

Chapter Five

Brace your backbone and forget your wishbone.
> —Traditional cowboy saying

"Eeee, doggie!"

A yell echoed through Miley's suite and penetrated the fog of sleep. "What time is it?" she moaned. She opened one bleary eye and saw Lilly stretched out on her bed a few feet away. Lilly looked just as bleary-eyed as Miley.

"What's going on?" Lilly yawned. "Is this some kind of Texas wake-up call?"

"Worse," Miley muttered. She pulled her pillow over her head. "It sounds like Dad."

Any hope Miley had of getting back to sleep was shattered when another cowboy yodel rang through the air, followed by a rapid pounding on the door. "Miley! Lilly!" Mr. Stewart yelled. "Rise and shine! I've got news that'll blow the barn door open!"

Miley threw her pillow on the floor and looked at Lilly, shrugging. "We might as well," she sighed. "You know how he is when he's got barn-door-blowing news."

"I would ask you to translate that," Lilly said groggily, "but I don't think it would make any more sense if I were awake."

They rolled out of their beds, pulled on their robes, and staggered out into the suite's living room. Jackson and Oliver were already seated at the table, eating a room-service breakfast. There were three breakfast plates still untouched, one for Miley, one for Lilly, and one for Mr. Stewart, who was ignoring his breakfast in favor of pacing back and forth. Every few steps, he'd stop to reread a piece of paper he was holding. After scanning it with undisguised glee, he would laugh to himself, shake his head, and start pacing again.

"Good. You finally decided to join the land of the living," Jackson said through a mouthful of pancakes. "Maybe now we can find out what's such a big deal that we had to hear a hillbilly yell at eight o'clock in the morning!"

"Mr. Stewart said we had to get up and come up to your suite to hear some big news," Oliver said, stabbing a sausage with his fork. His hair was rumpled, and his shirt was on inside out. "Right away, he said! It couldn't wait, he said!" Oliver eyed Miley and Lilly accusingly. "And then he wouldn't tell us anything until *you* managed to crawl out of bed."

"And I'm sure as shootin' glad you finally showed up," Mr. Stewart said, "'cause I'm too gol'darn excited to keep this inside any longer!"

"Warning, warning," Miley muttered to Lilly. "Major Enthusiasm Alert. Level five, at least."

"It's too early for level five," Lilly moaned in response. "We haven't even had breakfast."

Mr. Stewart stopped in midstep and whipped the cover off a room-service tray. "There you go, girls," he said. "Eggs, bacon, toast, juice . . . now are you ready to hear my news?"

Miley grabbed the last piece of wheat toast, getting there a millisecond before Lilly. Lilly made a face at her and nabbed the juice.

"Okay, Dad," Miley said through a buttery bite of whole wheat. "What's so important we couldn't sleep in for another fifteen minutes?"

"I got selected as a contestant in the Lone Star Rodeo Official Barbecue Competition!" her dad shouted. "Can you believe it? I'm going to go up against the best of the best when it comes to barbecue!"

"Congratulations, Dad." Miley was genuinely pleased for her father. For one thing, she liked to see him happy. For another thing, every minute he spent barbecuing was one less minute he could spend watching their every move. "That's awesome."

"You know it," her dad grinned. "Five rounds of finger-lickin' good competition! And at the end, maybe, just maybe"—his voice dropped to an awed whisper—"I'll be taking home . . . the *Golden Brisket.*"

Miley, Lilly, Oliver, and Jackson exchanged uncomprehending stares. "The what?" Miley asked.

"The Golden Brisket!" her dad said, clearly astonished that he had to explain this. "It's the most coveted trophy in the international world of grilling cook-offs!"

"Huh," Jackson said. "And to think that all those silly people in Hollywood get excited about winning an Oscar."

Mr. Stewart glared at him. "This *is* an Oscar, son," he said. "The Oscar of barbecue."

"But really, Dad, the Golden Brisket?" Miley said. "Where'd they get that name? Why not call it the Platinum Pulled Pork?"

"Or the Silver Spare Rib?" Jackson suggested, getting in the spirit of things.

"Or the Crystal Kielbasa?" Miley snickered.

Their father shook his head. "And I thought I raised you children right," he said mournfully.

"Well, I think it sounds cool, Mr. Stewart," Lilly chimed in. "Really."

"Cool? *Cool*? It's more than cool." Mr. Stewart placed his hand reverently over his heart. "It's what every grill jockey dreams of."

Jackson broke into this misty-eyed moment without ceremony. "That's great, Dad," he said. "But how can you compete? Ol' Bessie's back in Malibu." His face darkened as he remembered, for the umpteenth time, the grievance that he was still nurturing in his heart despite some of the perks he was getting on this trip. "Remember Malibu? The place we could be right now, doing some California dreaming instead of all this Texas two-stepping?"

Mr. Stewart's face clouded over. "You're

right, son! I'm stranded up a creek without a paddle! I'm stuck high and dry! I'm—"

"Thinking you should get ol' Bessie on a truck so she'll be here in time," Miley finished for him.

"That's a great idea, Miley," her dad said. "But a truck might take too long. And Bessie won't like being bounced around. . . . I know!" He snapped his fingers. "I'll just buy her a plane ticket!"

Jackson sighed, got up, and put his hand on his father's shoulder. "I hate to be the one to break it to you, old man," he said, "but you've officially gone off the deep end. A plane ticket? For a grill?"

"You betcha," Mr. Stewart said. He was in a much happier mood now that he'd thought of a way to get his grill to Texas. "First class, as a matter of fact."

Everyone stared at him in disbelief.

"What?" he said. "Are you saying Bessie doesn't deserve it?"

"Oh, no," Lilly said hastily.

"Not at all," Oliver added.

"Brilliant idea," Miley said. "In fact, you'd better call the airline right away to make arrangements. You know how fast those first-class seats sell out."

She exchanged a quick, conspiratorial glance with Lilly, who immediately picked up on her cue.

"And you'd better get started making your super-secret-and-special sauce!" Lilly chimed in. "You'll need barrels of it to last through all those rounds!"

Mr. Stewart started pacing again. "That's true," he said. "Ol' Bessie's a champ, but she's going up against the big dogs now! I've got to make sure she has everything she needs in order to win."

"You need to spend every minute possible fine-tuning that award-winning sauce," Miley urged him. "You need to stay focused every minute if you want to win."

Finally, Jackson saw where his sister was going with this, and he had to admit, he liked it. He liked it a lot.

"Yeah, Dad, don't worry about us at all," he chimed in. "We'll just hang out, do our own thing, and, of course, not get into any trouble whatsoever."

Mr. Stewart stopped in midstride. He narrowed his eyes at his kids. "You wouldn't be trying to get rid of your old dad, would you?" he asked. "So that you can go off who-knows-where and get up to who-knows-what kinds of shenanigans?"

"Daddy!" Miley opened her eyes wide, hoping to look innocent. "How can you *think* such a thing?"

"I can think it because I know what young'uns are like," he said. "I used to be one, ya know."

"Long, long ago," Jackson said.

"In a galaxy far, far away," Miley chimed in.

"Uh-huh." He was not impressed with

their attempt at humor. "Any time you two agree on something, I get as nervous as a cat in a rocking-chair factory."

"It's okay, Daddy, we can take care of ourselves," Miley said, trying to sound earnest and responsible.

He gave her a long look, then nodded.

"Okay, you kids need to meet Jim Bob in the lobby in an hour," Mr. Stewart said. "He's taking y'all to the children's hospital for a visit. Jackson, I expect you to act like a fan."

"Dad!"

"And I expect you to watch out for your sister, understand?" he added.

Jackson's face lit up with evil delight. "Yes, sir," he said solemnly. "Don't you worry about a thing. I'll watch over my little sister every minute! I won't take a break during the day or get a wink of sleep at night! I'll do just as good a job of keeping tabs on her as you would if you were here!"

Mr. Stewart nodded, satisfied. "And Miley,

I expect you to be sweet to your brother. Acting like your biggest fan is real hard on him, and you don't need to rub it in. At least, not too much."

"Yes, Daddy," Miley said, but there was a wicked glint in her eye.

"So I can trust y'all to act right while I'm busy with my barbeque?" he asked. "I can depend on y'all to stay out of trouble while I'm gearing up to grill? I can rest easy—"

"That we'll be good while you're setting up your sauce," Jackson finished, rolling his eyes.

Mr. Steward glared at him. "Exactly my question," he said. "Well?"

Miley and Jackson looked at each other. It was a look of complete understanding and, for once, absolute sibling solidarity.

"Of course, Dad," they said in union. "You can count on us."

Chapter Six

Just 'cause trouble comes visiting doesn't mean you have to offer it a place to sit down.

—Traditional cowboy saying

"Hannah! Hannah! Over here! Give us a smile!"

On the inside, Miley sighed. Even after a good breakfast, the morning was still a little too new and she was still a little too sleepy to face the press.

On the outside, however, she dutifully gave her megawatt Hannah Montana smile as she stepped out of the limousine Jim Bob had hired to take her out to the trail ride, along with Lilly, Oliver, and Jackson.

A series of flashes went off. Camera motor drives whirred. And Jim Bob, who was now standing next to her, his arm around her shoulders, beamed.

Miley had already spent two full days as Hannah Montana, giving interviews for local reporters, visiting the children's hospital, and posing for pictures with members of the rodeo's organizing committee. She was already thinking longingly about tomorrow, when Hannah Montana would have her one and only full day off. Her dad's grill had arrived on an overnight flight, and he had been busy ever since trying out different sauce recipes. She would be free to explore the fairgrounds with Lilly and Oliver—and even, if absolutely necessary, Jackson.

But that was tomorrow, she reminded herself firmly. And today, she still had a lot of work to do.

Her first official duty had started shortly after dawn, when Jim Bob had picked them up and driven them for almost an hour into the Texas countryside to meet the trail ride. Now they were standing on the side of a dusty road along with a line of covered wagons that stretched all the way to the horizon. A dozen riders on horseback trotted up and down the side of the road. They wore cowboy hats and chaps and had bandanas tied around their necks and spurs on their boots. It looked like a scene right out of the nineteenth century— except for the small cluster of reporters and photographers, and the TV crew that had followed Hannah Montana's limo in search of a good story.

After a few more flashes, Jim Bob good-naturedly shooed the press off to the side so that he could escort Hannah toward a small group of saddled horses.

"You'll be on the front page of every newspaper in Texas tomorrow morning," Jim Bob said happily. "I bet we're going to set a new attendance record this year, thanks to you!"

Miley smiled politely. "That's real nice of you," she said, her Southern accent thickening. "But I just feel lucky to be here. Texas fans are the best in the world."

There was a snicker somewhere behind Miley's left shoulder. It was a snicker that she would have recognized anywhere, even if she heard it on Mars. Miley kept her smile plastered on her face and braced herself.

"Oh, you're being far too modest, Hannah Montana!" Jackson said. His voice was oily with fake sincerity, and his eyes glinted with fake enthusiasm. "We, the millions of Hannah Montana fans, are the ones who are lucky! Because we get to see you, Hannah Montana, perform live and in person!"

Miley turned her head away from the cameras to give him the Look of Death. During the course of their long car ride, Jackson had started amusing himself by trying to work the name "Hannah Montana" into every sentence, the more boring the better. As in, "Oh, look, Hannah Montana, there's a field! And can you believe it, Hannah Montana, there's a *cow* in the field! And check it out, Hannah Montana, the cow is eating *grass* in the field!"

Miley couldn't believe that no one else had picked up on Jackson's obvious sarcasm, but then the rest of the world had remained happily ignorant of her brother's presence . . . until now. Jim Bob, for example, was smiling at Jackson with evident approval. A couple of reporters jotted down that ridiculous quote. And the TV cameraman even turned his lens on Jackson and zoomed in on his face as he spoke.

"That's real sweet of you," Miley said as Oliver and Lilly both emerged from the limo and stood blinking in the blazing sunlight. "But you're embarrassing me." She moved a little closer so she could look him right in the eye. "Knock it off."

"I would, Hannah Montana, but my

feelings of admiration and respect for you are just too overwhelming!" he cried. "And my friend Oliver here feels the same way! Don't you, Oliver?"

"Um, yeah, I guess." Oliver looked from Jackson, who was grinning at him in an encouraging way, to Miley, who was glaring at him in a very *dis*couraging way. He quickly decided that the safest course of action was to remove himself from this sticky situation altogether.

"Hey, what's that great smell?" he asked, theatrically sniffing the air.

"Well, son, I do believe that's what's left of the chuck-wagon breakfast," Jim Bob said. He sniffed the air, too. "Homemade biscuits and apple butter, if I'm not mistaken, with some crispy fried bacon on the side. There might be a smidgen left if you boys are still hungry. . . ."

Oliver and Jackson grinned at each other. As much fun as it was to needle Miley—and despite having wolfed down an enormous breakfast only an hour ago—Jackson couldn't resist the lure of biscuits and bacon. And Oliver was always hungry. He and Oliver made a beeline for the chuck wagon.

Now that Jackson was gone, Miley finally got a chance to take in a little more of the scene around her.

Despite the heat, which was hovering in the nineties, and the blazing sun, everyone seemed to be in a great mood. Kids and dogs were chasing one another around the wagons. The sound of jingling bridles and horses' whinnies filled the air.

A smile of pure happiness lit up Miley's face. Everything about this scene felt so comfortable, so much like home. She almost wished that she didn't have to make an appearance as Hannah Montana and then head back to her rodeo duties. It would have been so much fun to hang out with the trail riders, wearing old jeans and a comfortable T-shirt instead of her pop-star clothes.

Of course, she'd kept her outfit informal for the trail-ride visit: her best jeans, white cowboy boots with blue embroidered flowers, and a cropped turquoise jacket over a white tank top. Still, there was no denying the fact that she stood out in this crowd, especially since she had on full makeup, and the jacket was decorated with sequins that glittered in the sunlight.

She glanced at Lilly, who was dressed in her Lola disguise. Today that meant a green wig, a gauzy pink top and jeans, a blinged-out necklace, and three rings on each hand. Thanks to the expression of pure terror on her face, she looked even more out of her element than Miley.

The reason for Lilly's terrified expression stood about five feet away—and about sixteen hands high. "Don't you worry none, little lady!" Jim Bob cried. "Midnight Mayhem won't bite."

Lilly edged a little farther away from the

large black horse standing on the side of the road. She gave Miley a wild look. "Then why is he called Midnight *Mayhem*?" she whispered.

"It's probably just a nickname," Miley whispered back in a soothing tone.

"Great," Lilly said. "Aren't nicknames based on key character traits? What do you think that horse did to earn a name that means 'absolute chaos and destruction'?"

Before Miley could answer, Jim Bob called out, "And we got a real sweet little horse for you, Hannah! Name of Bold Bandit!"

"Great," Lilly muttered. "It sounds like we're in some kind of superhero movie. Midnight Mayhem versus Bold Bandit in a battle to the death!"

"Thanks, Jim Bob!" Miley called out, keeping a bright smile on her face. "I'll be right there!" Out of the corner of her mouth, she muttered, "Buck up, Lola! I've been around horses my whole life. I'll help you out."

"Great. How about you help me out of here?" Lilly muttered back as she reluctantly followed Miley over to where the horses were standing and occasionally stamping the ground.

"Let me introduce you to this fine fellow," Jim Bob said to Lilly. He was stroking Midnight Mayhem's neck. Lilly had to admit, despite his name, the horse didn't look particularly fierce.

Lilly edged over to the large black horse, which lowered its head and whinnied. She jumped and let out a little scream.

The horse nibbled on her hair.

"Aagh!" Lilly yelled. She darted back to Miley's side, one hand clapped protectively over her wig. "He tried to bite me!"

"He was just nuzzling you," Miley said, reassuringly. "That means he likes you," she added.

Lilly was not convinced. "Or it means that he wants to eat my hair!"

Jim Bob gave the wig a long, considered

look. "Well, it does look a lot like grass, honey," he pointed out. "You can't blame Mayhem for getting a mite confused."

Miley was already standing next to Bold Bandit and stroking his nose. "Hey, there, fellow, you're a good boy, aren't you?" she crooned to the horse. "You're a sweetheart, yes, you are!"

Lilly watched this public display of affection with disbelief. "Um, Mi—I mean, Hannah, don't you think you should be saving that for someone else? Like, I don't know . . . a human boy?"

"Come on, Lola," Miley said. "Give Midnight Mayhem another chance."

But her friend, normally so brave and fearless, was eyeing the horse with a look of true fright on her face. "I'm sorry," Lilly whispered. "Why don't you get on your horse for the photo, and I'll meet you back at the car?"

Miley knew she should be sympathetic.

After all, she was a scaredy-cat when it came to a lot of things that Lilly loved to do, like skateboarding and surfing and inline skating.

On the other hand, she had always been willing to at least *try* all those things. Memories of scraped knees, scary waves, and one badly twisted ankle flooded into her mind. Yes, she had tried all those things, and she had paid the price! And why? Because she was Lilly's friend!

And now the tables were turned, and she was asking Lilly to step into her world for a little while—and Lilly was ready to give up without even trying! Which was too bad, Miley thought, because she *knew* that Lilly would love riding if she'd just give it a chance. . . .

So Miley blurted out the three words that she knew would get Lilly up on that horse, no questions asked. "I dare you!"

Lilly's eyes widened in shock. "You . . . what?" she gasped.

"In fact, I double-dog dare you!" Miley added with a challenging grin.

"You're on, sister!" Sure enough, Lilly's mouth tightened with determination as she grabbed the horse's bridle and catapulted herself into the saddle with ease. Once she was up there, high above the ground, she looked around, both shocked and pleased at what she had done. "Hey, you're right. This isn't so bad."

"Told you." Smiling, Miley mounted her own horse. Bold Bandit danced sideways for a few steps, but she clucked to him and he calmed down. "You ready to ride?"

Lilly's smile faded; her expression was unsure. "Ride? Hey, I'm *on* the horse, why do I have to *move* the horse?"

Miley chuckled. "Moving's the best part. Come on, I'll show you—"

But she was interrupted by the chuck wagon, which came rattling up the road to stop next to her. A voice called out in an exaggerated country accent, "Well, hey there, if it isn't Hannah on a horse."

"Jackson!" Miley's head swung around, and she glared at her brother. He was perched on the driver's seat with Oliver, who was holding the horse's reins in his hands.

"None other." Jackson touched the brim of his cowboy hat with his finger and smiled cockily at her. "Well, now, you sure do look purty today, Miss Hannah!"

"Stop it!" she hissed. "You sound like an idiot!"

"Really?" He pretended to be hurt. "And here I thought I sounded like Hannah Montana's number one fan." He paused as if thinking this over, then slapped his forehead. "Gol' darn it! I *do* sound like an idiot!"

"Very funny," Miley snapped. "And what are you doing with that wagon?" An awful thought struck her. "You didn't steal it, did you?"

"Yeah, I did, actually," Jackson said, deadpan.

"We're just hoping we can outrun the posse that's on our trail—"

"Very funny," Miley said, frowning. "Laugh now, because in the future you are going to be *so* grounded."

"It's okay." Oliver leaned forward to nod reassuringly at her. "We met the chuck wagon cook, and he said we could take his baby out for a spin. Although that makes it sound like we're spinning along, but it's really kind of bumpy and slow . . ."

A grizzled head popped out of the back of the wagon. "It's a wagon, you little whipper-snapper, not a sports car!" the man growled, frowning, his bushy gray whiskers making him look ferocious. "And remember, it's not a free ride, either."

Jackson rolled his eyes. "Meet my new best friend, Dub. Chief cook and bottle washer—"

"And owner of this here wagon, which I am only letting you drive in return for helping me clean up the breakfast dishes," Dub said. "*And* shell all these peas I got back here for lunch."

"Oh, yeah, the peas." A sly expression appeared on Jackson's face. "And we will do all that, we absolutely will. Right, Oliver?"

"Sure. I can't wait!" Oliver said with real enthusiasm. "Dub was just telling me that he's going to show us how to pop each pea pod open with just your thumb—"

"Yeah, great, sounds exciting, can't wait," Jackson interrupted. "Of course, we won't have too much time to learn about pea-shelling tricks, since we'll have to hop back in that limo and get back to the big city before you know it."

Dub's eyes widened, and his whiskers seemed to bristle with outrage. "Oh, no. I can spot the signs of a double-dealing lowdown snake when I see them. You're going to back out on our deal!"

"I don't *want* to, Dub, honest I don't,"

Jackson said earnestly. "But I *also* gave my word that I would stick close to Hannah Montana. See, I'm her biggest fan in the world, and I have to be next to her every minute of the day to make sure she's all right."

The trail cook jumped out of the wagon and stalked up to the front. He was short and bow-legged and looked so much like every trail cook in every old Western movie ever made that Miley suspected he had actually been hired by central casting.

His grumpy nature, however, seemed absolutely genuine. "Let me tell you something, boy," Dub yelled, shaking his finger at Jackson. "Out West, a man's word is his bond! There's a code among cowboys, and if you break it you're betraying the brotherhood of the trail!"

The reporters, attracted by the yelling and by the possibility of a juicy story involving Hannah Montana, pushed past Jim Bob and crowded around the scene that was unfolding.

Oliver looked worried. "Dub has a good point," he said to Jackson. "We don't want to break the cowboy code."

"We're not going to break it," Jackson said irritably. "We're just going to bend it a little."

"You rapscallion! You gol' darned little whippersnapper!" Dub's face was turning red.

The photographers moved in closer and started jostling for position.

Lilly let out a little shriek as her horse shied away from them.

"Sit up and pull back, Lilly," Miley called out to her. She didn't have a chance to see if her friend followed her advice, because her own horse was getting jumpy from the sudden influx of people, especially since the photographers had raised their cameras, thrusting them closer to the horse's head.

"Hannah! Look over here! Can we get a smile, Hannah?"

Without thinking, Miley sat up a little

straighter in her saddle and smiled, tossing her head so that the sun glinted off her hair. One photographer in particular, a woman with a wild mop of curly red hair, elbowed the TV cameraman to the side and moved in even closer.

"Can you turn this way, Hannah?" the woman yelled.

Miley turned her head as Midnight Mayhem moved a little closer to Bandit, as if hoping for protection in numbers. Miley just had time to notice Lilly's strained smile and pale face when the photographer lifted her camera even higher.

"Perfect!" she yelled. "Hold it—"

The camera flash went off right in Midnight Mayhem's face.

The horse whinnied and reared up. Miley saw Lilly fall off just as the horses pulling the chuck wagon also whinnied, clearly unnerved by all the commotion. Before she had a chance to dismount and go to Lilly, she heard Jackson yell, "Hold on! Stop! I mean, whoa!"

Her head snapped around, and she saw the back of the chuck wagon as it hurtled down the road, scattering reporters and photographers in its wake.

Then she heard Dub yell, "We got a runaway!"

And she saw Jackson and Oliver disappear in a cloud of dust.

Chapter Seven

If you find yourself in a hole, the first thing to do is stop diggin'.

—Traditional cowboy saying

"We're going to die!" Oliver screamed. "Help! Somebody! Anybody! We're going to diiiiiiiie!"

"Shut it, Oliver!" Jackson snapped, pulling back on the reins as hard as he could. "You're not helping!"

"What do you mean I'm not helping? Didn't you hear what I just said?" Oliver replied, his voice tinged with indignation. He leaned over to yell his message right in Jackson's ear, with a pause in between each word, just to make sure the meaning was clear. "We. Are. Going. To. Die!"

"Thanks for the news bulletin, Oliver!" It occurred to Jackson that maybe he should try telling the horses to stop, instead of relying on his own nonexistent horse-driving skills. Otherwise, Oliver's prediction might come true. It was worth a try, Jackson thought. "Whoa!" Jackson yelled. "Stop! Hold on!"

Still, the horses kept rocketing along.

"Who trained these horses?" Jackson said. "Don't they understand English?"

Oliver seized on this with the fervor of a desperate man. "Maybe they're Spanish speakers!" he said. He had started taking Spanish in high school. Now he searched his memory for the right word, silently berating himself for not paying more attention to Senora Johannsen when he'd had the chance, before he was facing imminent death. . . .

Plato? No, that meant plate.

Padre? No, that meant father.

It was a word that started with a *p*, he was sure of it. . . .

Finally, he got it.

"*Parada!*" he screamed.

But the horses apparently didn't understand Spanish any better than they understood English, because they didn't stop. If anything, Oliver's voice seemed to spur them on to run even faster.

"Isn't there a brake on this thing?" Oliver's voice had an edge of hysteria. "I'm sure there is some governmental regulation that requires an emergency brake on any covered wagon meant to be used for transportation purposes. . . ."

Jackson ignored Oliver's babbling and resorted to pleading with the horses. "Please, do me this one little favor. At least slow down a little bit . . ."

"Oh, no! Look! Up ahead!"

Jackson glanced up and saw the intersection of two major roads, with dozens of cars whizzing past.

Even as Jackson faced his sure and certain doom, he had a millisecond to wish that he was inside one of those cars—one of those sweet, twenty-first-century cars that obeyed a driver's commands—instead of here, at the mercy of four panicked horses without enough brains among them to figure out that it wasn't a great idea to gallop into traffic. . . .

Then, seemingly out of nowhere, a rope flashed through the air. The loop of the lasso landed right on the neck of one of the lead horses.

A voice called out, "Whoa!" with far more authority than Jackson could dream of mustering up.

And then, in less time than Jackson would have thought possible, the horses slowed to a trot and finally stopped. They stood on the side of the road, their sides heaving. The mysterious rider trotted up, took the lasso off the horse, then turned back to where Jackson and Oliver were sitting.

"Thank you," Oliver said fervently. "Thankyouthankyouthankyouthankyou. . . ."

Jackson elbowed him in the ribs to stop his babbling. "Yeah, thanks for your help," he said, trying to sound cool. "Of course, I had everything under control, but it was nice of you to step in."

The rider pushed back the brim of a cowboy hat and looked straight at Jackson.

His mouth dropped open. Their rescuer was . . . a girl!

She had stern gray eyes and brown hair tied back in a neat braid. Her lip curled slightly as she looked him over. "Yeah, I could see you had everything under control," she said. "I especially liked the way you were heading for a major intersection. Real bold move there, cowboy."

Jackson's mouth dropped open. He knew she was being sarcastic, he could hear it in her voice, but his heart jumped anyway. He knew she scorned him, he could see it in her eyes, but he was finding it hard to breathe all the same. He knew she probably didn't want to have anything more to do with him, he could sense it by the way she was already looking away, waving to the people who were hurrying over to see if they were all right—but he didn't care.

Jackson was completely, utterly, smitten.

"So, you must have been riding for a long time, huh?"

Now that the excitement about the runaway wagon was over and everyone had returned to the campsite, the trail riders were getting packed up to start on the day's journey. Jackson was flitting around behind his rescuer, trying to get her attention. This wasn't easy to do, as she was busy checking the other horses' saddles, packing away her bedroll, and helping Dub stow the pans used to make breakfast.

Still, Jackson wouldn't give up.

"Where do you live? How did you learn to

use a lasso like that? And, hey, what's your name, anyway?"

She stopped in the middle of shoving a box aside in the back of the covered wagon and turned to give him a level look. "My name's Lizzy Lee Landers," she said crisply. "I'm from Alpine, I've been rodeoing since I was eight, and I'm very busy. So would you please mind moving?"

Jackson just stared at her with an idiotic grin. To be truthful, very little of what she had said had even penetrated his brain. He was lost in a fog of love. Finally, though, he did notice that she was looking at him, one eyebrow raised in a way that said she had asked a question and was waiting for an answer. Jackson quickly searched his short-term memory to see if he could retrieve what that question was. . . . Nope. He had no idea. So he fell back on a useful reply, suitable for many occasions. "What?"

Lizzy Lee sighed impatiently. "I *said*,

move," she repeated. "I'm leading the trail ride today. I need to get mounted up."

"Oh! Sure! No problem!" Jackson said, not moving.

She shook her head, then shoved past him to get to her horse.

"Hey, listen, my name's Jackson," he said, scurrying after her. "I'm from Malibu. You know, in California?"

Lizzy Lee stopped and turned to look at him. "Malibu? Where all the movie stars hang out?"

"Yeah, exactly!" Jackson said eagerly.

Her face darkened. "I hate movie stars." She kept walking.

"Oh." Jackson was taken aback, but only for a moment. He hurried after her. "Well, hey, listen, how do you feel about pop stars? Do you like Hannah Montana? 'Cause I'm really tight with her; in fact, I came out here in her limo—"

"Oh, right, I saw that car," Lizzy Lee said,

swinging herself up into the saddle.

"Pretty slick, huh?" Jackson asked, puffing his chest out a little with pride.

She made a face. "It stuck out like a stinkbug in a flour bin," Lizzy Lee said. "This is a trail ride, not a fancy-dress party. But maybe you didn't notice that, since you're from *Malibu*." She said the last word as if she'd bitten into a lemon.

"Hey, I'm from Tennessee originally," Jackson said. "I couldn't wait to get away from the beach and the ocean and, um, all that traffic! All this . . ." He swept his arm in a circle to indicate the pastures on either side of the road, the horses, and the wagons, his face a picture of bliss. "It reminds me of when I was a kid, growing up in the country."

"Right." Lizzy Lee looked down at him, her expression skeptical. "If you'll pardon me saying so, you seem more like a city boy."

"A city boy who wants to get back to his country roots," Jackson said craftily. "If only there was someone who could help me . . ."

Lizzy Lee's cool gaze rested on him for a moment. "Uh-huh. You just keep working on that. But, in the meantime, stay out of my way." She picked up her reins and started down the road, turning back to call over her shoulder. "'Cause I don't like city boys. Especially when they try to pull the wool over this country girl's eyes. Giddyup, Rosie!"

Jackson blinked, and she was gone.

"I'm not going back."

"What?" Miley was standing by the limo with Lilly. When Jackson hurried over, they were waiting for Jim Bob to round everyone up so that they could get on the road.

"I'm not going back to the hotel," he elaborated. "I'm staying here. With the trail ride."

"You're kidding." She took a closer look at her brother. He looked pale and determined and . . . *serious*. Jackson? Serious? She felt a jolt of alarm and walked a few steps away from the car so that no one would overhear them. Lilly followed. "What's wrong?"

"Nothing." He shrugged, trying to look casual, but his eyes were darting around in that shifty way that let Miley know he was hiding something. "I just think it would be fun to ride with them for a few days. You know, really get into the spirit of the Old West. And, um, all that kind of stuff."

Miley and Lilly exchanged skeptical glances as Oliver came hurrying over.

"Hey, we should all stick around," he said. "Dub said he'd show me how to set up camp when the trail riders stop for the night. Did you know he can actually make shrimp scampi *and* peach cobbler over the campfire using just an old tin can and a branding iron? I'd really like to see that, wouldn't you?"

"You mean you'd really like to *eat* that," Lilly said. "Oliver, don't you ever think about anything except your stomach?"

"Hey!" Oliver protested. "Just because I have a sense of curiosity about the world—"

"Which is an excellent trait, by the way," Jackson interrupted. "You're absolutely right, Oliver."

"I am?" Oliver's mouth dropped open in astonishment.

Dub came running up, his face red with anger.

"There you are!" he yelled at Jackson. "Thought you'd pull one over on ol' Dub, did you? Figured you'd be halfway down the highway before I noticed you were gone, did you? Thought you'd get in that limo and skedaddle, leaving ol' Dub high and dry!"

Miley was watching Jackson closely, so she saw a crafty look cross his face. She waited, knowing that he had just hatched a new scheme, and she wondered how this one would backfire.

But she was surprised when he finally answered Dub. "You're right," Jackson said humbly. "I was thinking only of myself, and I totally forgot about my promise. But that's not right, Dub."

Dub raised his eyebrows, surprised. "No, it's not," he said. Then he lowered his eyebrows and glared at Jackson. "But I wouldn't expect you to cotton on to that fact. What are you up to, boy?"

Good question, Miley thought. She cast a bright, expectant look Jackson's way. She couldn't wait to hear the answer.

"Nothing!" Jackson said. "I'm simply making a sincere pledge to stay with this trail ride until I've fulfilled my promise."

"Really?" Miley asked. He had meant it?

"Yes!" Jackson put a hand over his heart. "And I'm shocked—*shocked!*—that you would expect anything less of me!"

Miley looked at Lilly. Lilly looked at Oliver. Oliver looked at Jackson.

"Awesome!" Oliver said. "Come on, let's get that peach cobbler going."

Miley met Lilly's eyes and saw the same incomprehension that she was feeling. Then she thought about what this meant.

No Jackson hanging around, pretending to be Hannah Montana's number one fan.

No Jackson watching her every move, thanks to her dad's order to be protective—make that overprotective—of her.

And no Jackson teasing her just because she wanted to have an innocent conversation with, say, a cute guy who happened to raise pigs.

She gave him a brilliant smile. "You're a good man, Jackson," she said. "We'll see you in a few days."

As she danced back over to the limo, she was humming under her breath. Tomorrow, Jackson would be on the trail ride, her father would be focused on his barbecue, and she was going to have a day off. Life suddenly looked a whole lot brighter.

☆   ☆   ☆

But when Miley and Lilly got back to the rodeo arena, they discovered that Jim Bob had a few more items to cross off his schedule.

"We'll just whip through this food section, because we need to get Hannah over to tonight's dinner with the organizing committee," Jim Bob said, glancing at his watch. "But you can't miss the barbecue tent. The semifinals are going to be held tonight."

"Why does everybody make such a big deal about barbecue in Texas?" Lilly asked. "I mean, it *is* just meat cooked over a fire. How hard is that? Cavemen used to do it."

Jim Bob stopped to look at her, astounded. "If you have to ask that question," he said, "you've never tasted real barbecue."

Suddenly Lilly seemed to remember her role as Lola Luftnagle, globe-trotting socialite. "Of course not," she sniffed haughtily. "We, the Luftnagle family, that is, have a full-time French chef. Naturally. His name is, um, Pierre Saint-Sancerre. He's been working for our family for years and years. And Pierre *hates* barbecue."

Miley coughed, to stop Lilly before she got too carried away with creating a background that would explain Lola's ignorance of barbecue.

But Lilly kept rambling on. "So, of course, my knowledge of barbecue is very limited. Because of Pierre, you see, and his almost pathological dislike for outdoor cookers—ouch!"

She glared at Miley, who had just stepped on her toes. Hard.

Fortunately, Jim Bob didn't notice a thing. "Well, that Pierre guy would hate what we're about to see, then," he chuckled. "You know, I like to grill on weekends once in a while, but I admit I'm out of my league when it comes to these guys. Some of them even miss football games to go to barbecue competitions!"

"No!" Miley said, pretending to be shocked.

"Oh, yeah, I'm here to tell you, they

are *serious,*" he said. "Would you believe, some of them even give their grills names?"

"*Really.*" Lilly shook her head and grinned at Miley. "Some people are just obsessional, I guess."

For several minutes, Jim Bob led them through aisles crowded with smoking grills. He finally stopped at a battered and beaten grill that looked very familiar—for good reason. Mr. Stewart stood in front of it, a pair of tongs in one hand and a sauce brush in the other. His expression was serious and intense. He didn't even notice the small crowd that had started following Miley or the flashes from people taking pictures of Hannah Montana with their cell phones.

"Hello, sir," Jim Bob said. "I'd like to introduce you to one of the rodeo's celebrity hosts. I don't know if you happen to recognize this young lady—"

Mr. Stewart glanced up and jumped in surprise. "Hey, Mi—I mean, um, yes, I think

I've seen her somewhere before," he said. He squinted at Miley, a gleam of mischief in his eyes. "Now let's see, where would it have been? Are you one of those reality-show stars, maybe?" He pretended to think for a second, then snapped his fingers. "That's it! You're the one who broke down crying when she got kicked off that singing show for being off-key, right?"

Miley made a face at her dad and mouthed the words, *very funny*. Then she said, as sweetly as possible, "No, that wasn't me, but I'm not surprised you don't know me. After all, most of my fans are, well . . . *young*."

He made a face back at her as Jim Bob turned away for a moment, and she bit her lip to keep from laughing.

"Excuse me, can we have a little room here, please," Jim Bob said as more Hannah fans stopped to watch. "If you could all just take one big step back, that would be a help . . ."

As he moved away to deal with the crowd, Mr. Stewart said under his breath, "Where's Jackson? I thought he was going to watch out for you."

"Staying on the trail ride," she muttered back quickly. "Oliver's with him. Everything's fine."

He gave her a searching look. "I can count on you and Lilly to—"

"Act right. Stay out of trouble," she said, nodding. "Don't worry."

Before he could say anything else, Jim Bob returned, looking anxious. "We'll have to be heading back to the hotel in four minutes," he said. He nodded at Mr. Stewart. "Perhaps you could tell Hannah here a few of your grilling secrets?"

"Why, sure," Mr. Stewart said. Miley sighed as she recognized the faraway look in his eyes which meant that he about to launch into a lecture on charcoal management or temperature control. "Now I just got done searing, so I gotta move my chicklets off the heat. You see, it's important to move them away from the flame so they stay moist. That's the biggest mistake the beginning barbecuer makes. Of course, you've got to have a trust-worthy grill."

He patted the side of the grill. "And that's my real secret. Bessie's never let me down yet! Now, my other secret is my extraspecial sweet and sassy sauce." As he brushed more sauce on the meat, he began crooning to the chicken. "Oh, yeah, you like that sauce, don't you, my little chicklets, because it makes you so, so incredibly tasty. In fact, it makes you tasty enough to win a trophy—"

"Yes, well, that's fascinating," Miley interrupted loudly. The only thing worse than her dad bragging about his grill was when he started sweet-talking his chicken. "And that does smell delicious, but—"

"Why, thank you kindly," Mr. Stewart said. "Here, why don't you try a bite?"

Miley put the morsel of chicken in her mouth. Her dad was right. This was trophy tasty! She had almost finished when she realized that she was chewing in complete silence.

She glanced around. The crowd of people stared back at her expectantly.

She murmured to Jim Bob, "Um . . . why is everyone looking at me?"

"They want to hear your verdict!" he said, as if it should be obvious.

"But I'm not one of the barbecue judges," she said, confused.

"No, but you're Hannah Montana!" he said. "Everyone wants to know what you think, whether you're an official judge or not."

"Oh." Miley gulped and looked at her dad, who seemed to be holding his breath. "Well," she said finally, "I think . . . that's the best barbecue I've ever tasted."

Mr. Stewart beamed. The crowd applauded.

And then, to Miley's relief, Jim Bob took her elbow and announced loudly, "We've got another pressing appointment, so we'll have to be moving on. Excuse me, folks, coming through. . . ."

As Miley, Lilly, and Jim Bob walked toward the exit, the crowd of people clustered around Mr. Stewart and his grill, Bessie. They were snapping photos and asking tons of questions about his secrets for making the perfect, Hannah Montana–approved barbecued chicken.

"That was real nice of you to say you liked his chicken," Jim Bob said to Miley. "You know, a celebrity endorsement is probably worth more than a blue ribbon."

Miley met Lilly's eye, a little awed by this thought. "Wow," she said. "I never realized how much influence I have!"

But Lilly was too good a friend to let Hannah's fame go to Miley's head. She winked at Miley and whispered, "You must use this power only for good," her voice so solemn that Miley could only laugh and shrug sheepishly before following Jim Bob to the next stop on her schedule.

Chapter Eight

Don't wake a sleepin' rattler.

—Traditional cowboy saying

"Maybe we should go back to look at the 4-H exhibits," Miley suggested brightly to Lilly the next morning. They had decided over breakfast that they would spend Miley's day off exploring the fairgrounds. Now they were peeking into the hallway to make sure there wasn't anyone around who would see them leave Hannah Montana's suite. "That's always superfun!"

Lilly raised one eyebrow. "You mean all those pens filled with chickens and sheep and cows and, hmmm, what am I forgetting? Oh, right. Pigs. Pigs owned by cute boys?"

Miley blushed, but Lilly had already turned back to scan the hallway. "Okay, the coast is clear," she said, waving for Miley to follow her. As they ran down the hall to the stairs, Miley added, "Anyway, he *was* pretty cute."

"You're really interested in a guy who tries to get girls by roping them?" Lilly asked.

"What guy are you talking about?" Miley said innocently. "*I* was talking about the pig."

Laughing, they raced each other down the stairs.

"Hey," Miley said, smiling.

"Hey." The boy in the cowboy hat nodded to her.

Then they stood there, staring at each other.

Lilly sighed. Miley was clearly in the midst of a major crush. Lilly could recognize the signs. The first one was a complete inability to talk.

Well, Lilly was nothing if not a true friend. Before the silence could stretch to eternity, she stepped in. "Hey," she said, "I'm Lilly."

"Oh!" Miley seemed to wake up. "I'm Miley!"

"My name's Cash," he said.

"Hi!" Miley nodded her head so many times she looked like a bobblehead doll. Then she added brightly, "Nice pig!"

Lilly rolled her eyes. *Nice pig?* Mentally, she noted the second sign of a major crush: the inability to say anything sensible.

But Cash seemed to think this was a great conversation starter. In fact, his face lit up with enthusiasm as he said, "Thanks. I'm real proud of Sweet Pea. I've been raising pigs since I was eight years old, but he's the best one I've ever had. I've spent the last six months walking him every morning, cleaning out his pen every night, feeding him every morning and every night and sometimes in between—"

"He looks great." Miley leaned over the pen

to get a better look. "Did you feed him corn or grain?"

"Mostly corn. He seems to like it better." He reached down to scratch the pig's ears. "And yogurt, believe it or not. He loves that."

"Well, bless his heart!" Miley said. "He seems real spunky. Did y'all have problems with him cuttin' loose?" Miley asked.

Her drawl was becoming more pronounced, Lilly noticed. She chalked that up to the third sign of a major crush: an unconscious mimicking of the person you had a crush on. Lilly shuddered as she recalled the time she had fallen in love, ever so briefly, with Judson Green, whose favorite hobby was making artwork out of dryer lint. Only her extreme allergy to fabric softener had broken them up, and she still had a couple of lint still lifes in the attic.

Miley was still nattering on about pigs and flirtatiously twirling a lock of brown hair.

"We had a pig when I was little, and he was a natural-born escape artist. One time, he got out and had us all chasing him around the yard for an hour until I finally tackled him!"

Cash smiled. "I wish I could have seen that."

"I'm glad you didn't," Miley answered. "When I grabbed him, we fell right into his mud wallow. I had to take three baths to get all the dirt off."

He chuckled. "Sweet Pea isn't quite that bad, but then I fence him in pretty good."

"Really. What kind of pen did you build?"

Lilly shot a quick sideways glance at Miley. She couldn't believe it, but Miley sounded really interested . . . not just I'm-flirting-so-I'll-pretend-to-be-interested, either. Lilly tuned out Cash's answer—a long and detailed description that involved fence posts and cross braces—and looked more closely at the animal that seemed to have enthralled both Cash and Miley. Perhaps, if she looked long enough and hard enough, she could see what all the fuss was about.

The pig's little eyes met hers.

Lilly stared into them.

The pig stared back.

Lilly's competitive instincts kicked in. She had been the staring-contest champion in fifth grade. She had stared down the best, from Buddy Hollister to Samantha Folkeston to Chase Hunter. And if a porker named Sweet Pea thought that Lilly was going to look away, he had another think coming! Lilly narrowed her eyes to slits, the better to shoot out her laser glare, the one that left the competition reeling, the one that made her stare feared above all others at Seaview Elementary School. . . .

But Sweet Pea didn't even blink.

"Uh . . . Lilly? Are you okay?"

Startled, Lilly turned to see Miley watching her with concern.

"Fine!" she said quickly, embarrassed that

she had been caught having a staring contest with a pig, and, even worse, that she had just lost.

Behind her, she imagined she heard Sweet Pea grunt with satisfaction.

Thank goodness nobody in Malibu would ever hear about this, Lilly thought. She'd never live it down.

A little wave of homesickness swept through her at the thought of Malibu. She'd really been looking forward to going on this trip with Miley, but she didn't feel at home the way Miley did.

She was scared of horses.

She didn't like pigs.

And she was beginning to feel like a third wheel, standing there and saying nothing while Miley and Cash started talking about the ridin', ropin', and steer rasslin' they were going to see that night at the rodeo.

Lilly's lip trembled slightly. Not that she begrudged Miley the chance to flirt with someone like Cash—who was really cool, even if he did have a thing for pigs—but it would have been nice for her to meet someone, too. . . .

And just then, a boy with unruly dark hair ambled up to them. He was wearing old jeans, beat-up sneakers, and a faded T-shirt that read, CATCH BIGGER AIR IN TEXAS.

"Hey, Cash," he said. "Aren't you going to introduce me to your friends?"

"Gabriel, may I present Miley? Miley, Gabriel," Cash said, mock formally. "And this is Lilly. Lilly, Gabe is my oldest friend. I've known him since kindergarten, and so I feel real good about telling you to watch your step with him."

Lilly just stared at Gabe. After a few seconds, Miley elbowed her in the ribs, and Lilly realized that her mouth was hanging open. She closed it with a snap. The first sign of a crush, she thought hazily: the complete inability to speak.

"Hi," she managed to croak, right before

her mind went blank. Frantically, she tried to think of something else to say. Her eyes fixed on his T-shirt, which pictured a small graphic of a skateboard under the slogan. "Um . . . are you a skateboarder?"

She winced. The second sign of a crush: the inability to say anything sensible.

But Gabe didn't seem to notice. "You got that right," he said in a cheerful drawl. He leaned against Sweet Pea's pen and crossed his arms. "I like riding boards as much as I like riding horses."

"Really?" Lilly said, dubious. She leaned next to him and crossed her arms. "Don't you think skateboards are way better than horses? I mean, skateboards don't try to bite you—"

Miley coughed.

Lilly stopped, puzzled.

Miley deliberately looked down at Lilly's arms. Lilly looked down, too—then quickly uncrossed her arms and moved away from the pen, blushing.

Crush sign number three, she thought: unconsciously mimicking the person you had a crush on.

Fortunately, again Gabe didn't seem to notice, and Miley covered nicely by saying, "Lilly rode a horse for the first time yesterday, and she got thrown. But I'm sure she'd like riding if she gave it another try."

"Is that right?" Gabe seemed to think that over for a minute. "Well, if you'd like to learn how to ride a horse, I'd be glad to teach you."

Lilly gulped. Of course she'd like to spend more time with Gabe! On the other hand, this also meant spending more time with horses. . . .

Instantly, she weighed her options and made her decision.

"Sounds great," she said. "When can we start?"

◈ Chapter Nine

Don't squat with your spurs on.
—Traditional cowboy saying

Clang! Clang! Clang!

"Huh? What?" Jackson sat bolt upright and stared around wildly.

"Get up, boy, it's already nigh on six o'clock!" Dub shouted as he rang a cowbell approximately two inches from Jackson's ear.

"Six? In the morning?" Jackson asked in disbelief.

"Well, it's sure as shootin' not six o'clock at night." Dub cackled. He rang the bell one last time, then climbed back into the chuck wagon.

Jackson fell back on his bedroll. "I've heard

stories about this hour of the day," he said to the dark sky, "but I thought they were just *rumors.*"

He turned his head and saw Oliver on his right, huddled inside his bedroll. Oliver apparently could sleep through fire sirens, earthquakes and—most amazing of all—Dub's cowbell. Not only did Oliver not wake up, but he actually burrowed deeper into his sleeping bag and muttered something that sounded like, "But a trip to Mars will take forever!"

Jackson's own eyes drifted closed—just for five more minutes of sleep, he promised himself, or ten, at the most—but just then, Dub re-emerged from the back of the chuck wagon.

"Oh, no, you don't!" he snarled, beating a tin can with a spoon to emphasize his point. "You promised to help me make the biscuits this morning, so get out of that sleepin' bag."

Jackson blinked at him, his mind fuzzy with sleepiness. *Had* he promised to make biscuits?

He yawned. The influx of extra oxygen seemed to get his brain working again, and suddenly the memories flooded back: his insistence that he had to shell all Dub's peas before going back to the rodeo. His sudden interest in the intricacies of chuck wagon cooking techniques. His pledge that if Dub would just teach him how to make a meal over a campfire he would help out any way he could, even if it meant . . .

"Getting up before dawn's the only way to get a jump on the day," Dub said now, handing him a washcloth. "I've already filled a tub with water if you want to wash. But you better get a move on, because we have thirty-eight hungry people who are going to want to put the feed bag on in about"—he squinted at the horizon, where a faint line of pale sky indicated that the sun was about to rise—"half an hour."

Jackson groaned as he got to his feet. He hadn't thought through what his rash promise to help Dub would lead to, and he hadn't considered how he'd feel after a night sleeping on the ground.

As he limped to the back of the wagon to splash cold water on his face, he reflected bitterly that no one had ever told him how much he would have to sacrifice for true love.

"Hurry up, boy, get those pans in the wagon," Dub shouted. "We're about to head out."

Jackson wiped his forehead. He'd been working for three hours and it was getting hot, even though it was only nine o'clock in the morning. He didn't want to think about what the temperature would be like by afternoon.

And he *really* didn't want to think about spending the day with Dub. Jackson had a sneaking feeling that the cook was having a laugh—or a dozen laughs—at his expense. Dub kept making little comments about Jackson's work and then chuckling under his breath, a low, sarcastic "heh-heh-heh" that was really getting on Jackson's nerves.

"Hey, Jackson!" Oliver grinned at him as he helped shove a box of utensils into the wagon. "You're looking bright-eyed and bushy-tailed!"

"Stop it!" Jackson hissed.

"Stop what?" Oliver asked, bewildered.

"Stop saying all those corny country things," Jackson said. "You sound like my dad. Or like Dub."

Oliver looked affronted. "What's wrong with using colorful speech? It shows imagination and a flair for language."

Jackson loaded two more pots into the wagon. "What it shows is that you're going native, Oliver," he said under his breath. "If you don't watch out, by the time we get back to Malibu, you'll be wearing spurs and talking about how much you need a good woman."

"But I'm *always* talking about how I need a good woman," Oliver said. He tilted his head, thinking. "But you've given me an idea. Maybe spurs would help. . . ." He wandered off.

Dub came around the back of the wagon. "Now I'm gonna show you how to tie this canvas together," he said. "That's so we don't lose our pots and pans on the trail. Then I'm gonna teach you how to drive a team of horses. The hardest part is sitting on that wooden driver's box, but don't worry. Your butt'll get numb after the first hour. After that, the rest of the trip is easy as slippin' on a muddy creek bank. Then we'll make camp, and I'll show you how to peel three hundred potatoes in under fifteen minutes." Dub puffed out his chest in pride as he added, "I've been the Texas state champion in spud skinnin' three years in a row."

Jackson stared at Dub. A sense of doom enveloped him. "Wow," he finally said. "The excitement just never stops, does it?"

"You were the one who wanted to be on the trail ride," Dub answered with a twinkle in his eye. "Wanted to be on it so bad, you'd do just about anything. Now I wonder why that was? Could it have anything to do with a cute little filly named Lizzy Lee?"

Jackson decided to bluff. "I don't know what you're talking about."

"Sure you don't." Dub shook his head, still grinning, and ambled away. "Heh-heh-heh."

Just then, Oliver came back, beaming.

"Guess what?" he shouted. "Lizzy Lee talked to her dad, and he said he had a couple of extra horses in his string and that we could ride them! Isn't that cool?"

Jackson brightened immediately. Here was a chance to achieve two very important goals: get closer to Lizzy Lee—and as far as possible from Dub.

Jackson glanced over at the cook. "That would be great, Oliver, as long as it's okay with Dub," he said, using the ultrapolite voice that he used in the principal's office or when his dad threatened to ground him.

"Why, sure." Dub grinned at him. "You're after that girl like a duck after a june bug, ain't you, boy?"

Jackson glared at him. "I just like horseback riding," he said. "That's all."

"You just keep telling that story, boy, that's what you're good at," Dub said. "Heh-heh-heh."

Oliver looked from Dub to Jackson, bewildered. "What's he talking about, Jackson?"

"I have absolutely no idea," Jackson said. Then he hurried after Oliver to saddle up.

Jackson's mouth was parched. His face was sunburned. And every muscle in his body ached from spending hours on a horse.

And as the trail ride finally halted to make camp and Jackson gratefully slid out of his saddle to the ground, he had to admit to himself that, so far, his plan to charm Lizzy Lee Landers was a total bust.

True, he had managed to stay in his saddle, no small accomplishment considering that Lizzy Lee's father had put him on Buttons, a small, nervous, gray horse that startled easily. A squirrel darting across the road, the honk of a car horn, even a leaf blowing in the wind seemed to be enough to make Buttons dance in circles or even rear up.

And he secretly considered it rather impressive that, once Buttons settled down, he had managed to point her in the right direction and then keep her heading that way, rather than exploring the little side paths that she clearly preferred.

But when he had finally managed to maneuver his beast next to Lizzy Lee's, her huge brown horse had cast a disdainful look at him and Buttons and then pointed his muzzle straight ahead, as if he didn't even want to be associated with them.

"Howdy, little lady," he had said, hoping to get her to laugh. But Lizzy Lee just glanced sideways with an expression that was scarily similar to that of her horse.

"Don't even try it," she said.

"Try what?" Jackson asked, giving her his best innocent look.

"Don't try to be charming, don't try to win me over, don't try to convince me I should give you the time of day," she answered. "Just . . . *don't.*"

Buttons shimmied at the sight of a piece of trash on the side of the road. Jackson grabbed the pommel of his saddle just in time to keep his seat.

"Okay," he said gamely. "But you can't stop me from asking for your help, can you? I mean, given that I obviously could use all the help I can get?"

Jackson thought he saw the corner of her mouth lift in a slight smile. But then Lizzy Lee said, "You are a mess, that's for sure," and he realized he was probably imagining it.

It didn't help that Oliver trotted up right

then, looking as if he'd been born in the saddle. "Hey, Jackson. Hey, Lizzy Lee," he called out. "Do you want to see me gallop? Dub said he's never seen anyone learn to ride as fast as I have! He says I have a hidden talent! He says—"

But the rest of what Dub had to say about Oliver's horsemanship was lost when a car whizzed by and the driver honked his horn. It was probably supposed to be a friendly greeting, but Buttons didn't take it that way. Her eyes rolled wildly and she reared up.

Jackson just had time to yell, "Whoa!" before he fell off.

Lizzy Lee swung down out of the saddle and helped him to his feet. "You all right, cowboy? You're looking kind of puny."

"I'm fine," Jackson lied. In fact, he was quite shaken by his sudden re-acquaintance with the ground. He smiled, doing his best to look the exact opposite of puny. "Every cowboy's gotta take some spills now and then, right?"

Oliver chose this moment to offer some seasoned riding advice. "You've got to hold on," he said. "That way, you won't fall off."

Jackson glared at Oliver. "Thanks for that tip," he said through gritted teeth.

Lizzy Lee watched as Jackson tried to get back on the horse. It took him only three tries. When he was finally settled, she said, "Try gripping the horse tighter with your knees."

"Okay," he gasped. "Good idea."

She nodded and pulled her hat down over her eyes. "See you on the trail," she said, then cantered off.

The rest of the day had gone like that. His horse would try to buck him off, and he would throw his arms around the horse's neck to keep from falling. His horse would suddenly decide to run like the wind, and he'd try to stop her by pulling on the reins and yelling, "Whoa! Whoa!" as the other riders snickered. And every time Jackson turned around, he saw

Oliver trotting merrily along, chatting with everyone on the trail ride and having a great time.

Now, as Jackson wearily unsaddled his horse, all he could think about was crawling into his sleeping bag and closing his eyes.

Lizzy Lee cantered by, leaving a cloud of dust in her wake. Jackson coughed. Even through his watering eyes, he saw that she looked as fresh as when she had started that morning. He stared down at his own jeans, now dirty from several falls, and his shirt, sweat-stained from hours in the hot sun.

Dub saw him limping along and called out, "You look like something the cat drug in and the dog wouldn't eat."

"Thanks, Dub," Jackson said sarcastically. "Good to see you again, too."

Oliver popped out from behind the chuck wagon, carrying a coil of rope. "Guess what?" he cried. "Dub's going to teach me how to throw a lariat."

"Yee-haw." Jackson didn't try to hide the bitterness in his voice.

Dub's shrewd eyes darted from Jackson to Oliver, then back to Jackson. "Tell you what I'll do," Dub said. "I'll teach you both some roping tricks. That's a surefire way to get girls." He winked at Jackson. "Take it from me."

Jackson sighed. This is what my love life has come to, he thought. I'm getting tips from a chuck-wagon cook.

On the other hand, he hadn't done a very good job of impressing Lizzy Lee on his own. And he certainly didn't have any better ideas.

"All right," Jackson said, holding out his hand for the rope. "Show me what you've got."

Chapter Ten

Every trail has some puddles.
            —Traditional cowboy saying

The beauty pageant competition was being held in an auditorium on the rodeo grounds. When Miley, dressed as Hannah Montana, arrived for the interview portion of the pageant, the seats were already half-filled with friends and relatives of the contestants.

A few people saw her and gasped, then headed in her direction, searching through purses and backpacks for a pen and something that she could sign.

"Hold on, folks, there'll be plenty of time to get her autograph later," Jim Bob said, steering her firmly away from her fans and toward the backstage area.

"Oh, Mr. Cooper, come quick!" An elderly woman with a tape measure dangling around her neck rushed up, her face the picture of distress. "We have an evening-gown emergency! A pipe broke in one of the dressing rooms, and three gowns were soaked! I don't know what we'll do, I honestly don't. This is a tragedy, that's what it is, an absolute tragedy!"

He sighed and patted the woman on the arm. "Now, calm down, Miz Lila," he said. "I sure don't want you to get upset over something as trifling as a few little water stains. Let me see what I can do."

"Oh, thank you so much. I'll be in your debt forever and a day if you can fix this for us, I surely will," Miss Lila said, gazing up at him as if he were a knight in shining armor who had just ridden in to save them all from certain doom.

"Let me just introduce Miss Hannah to the other judges," he said. "I'll be right there."

While Miss Lila scurried off toward the dressing room, Jim Bob led Miley over to a group of people standing on the stage. Even from a distance, Miley could see Joshua McAdams, tilting his head just so in order to take advantage of the stage lights, which cast a golden halo around his head. He was holding court with a half dozen girls wearing banners across their chests.

"Yeah, the shoot for that video was totally exhausting," he was saying. "You know the big scene at the end, when I have to climb up that big oak tree in the middle of a thunderstorm?"

"I love that scene!" a short, red-haired girl gushed. Miley squinted at her banner. She was Miss Mississippi. "I play it all the time on my MP3 player! I mean, like, constantly!"

"You and four hundred thousand other people," he said complacently. "That video was the number one download for three weeks in a row. Anyway, we had to shoot it, like, a billion times because the rain machine kept breaking down. It was two in the morning before we finished."

"It was worth it," said Miss Rhode Island, a girl with long, curly black hair. *"Totally."*

"Well, thanks." Joshua modestly lowered his gaze, as if he were suddenly overcome by shyness. He even scuffed his foot back and forth on the floor. "That means so much to me. You have no idea."

The girls cooed with delight. Miley rolled her eyes. At least he's in a better mood now that he's surrounded by adoring fans, she thought.

"Mornin', everybody," Jim Bob said. "I'd like to introduce Hannah Montana—"

"Hey," Miley said with a smile. "Nice to meet y'all."

The girls' eyes widened with surprise and delight. Miss Mississippi actually let out a little squeal.

"I'd love to get your autograph!" Miss South Dakota said. Then she looked startled and cried, "Oh, I don't have anything to write on! And I don't have a pen!"

"Settle down now," Jim Bob said gently. "There'll be plenty of time for autographs later on. Right now, I think you girls need to go backstage and get ready for the interview competition, all right?"

The girls giggled and scurried off. Joshua watched them go, then turned his high-beamed smile on Miley. "It's great meeting you," he said. "I really enjoy your work."

"I like yours, too," Miley responded politely. And after all, she thought, that was true. His songs were great, and he was an awesome performer. It was a shame he wasn't a nicer guy. . . .

"I really didn't want to do this gig," he confided, as if to prove Miley's point. "I mean, come on! Singing at a rodeo? In Texas, of all places?" He shook his head in disbelief. "But you know how managers are. They get you hooked into things before you know it, and then it's impossible to back out." He sighed a long-suffering sigh, then moved an inch or two closer and looked deep into Miley's eyes. "But it'll be great to hang out with someone else who's in the business."

Ick, ick, and double ick, Miley thought, resisting the urge to back away.

"Hey, maybe we could go out tonight, once we're finished with the judging," he suggested.

"Actually, I already have plans," Miley said quickly. "Very important plans that have been on my calendar for a very long time and which I couldn't possibly cancel. You know how it is." She shrugged and tried to imitate his voice as she said, "*Managers.*"

He shrugged. "No biggie. Maybe tomorrow? There's not a lot of night life around here, but I heard about a restaurant that's supposed to be pretty good. I'm sure we'd get the VIP treatment."

"Um, well . . ."

Before Miley could come up with another

excuse, a voice interrupted. "Hannah Montana! I'm just so happy to meet you!"

Relieved, Miley turned around—to find Peyton standing in front of her, her eyes shining with excitement. "Oh, hi, P—" she began, then bit her lip.

You don't know who she is, Miley reminded herself. Look blank! Look blank!

Fortunately, Peyton was so caught up in introducing herself that she didn't notice Miley's near slip. "My name is Peyton Fredericks, and I am just your biggest fan!" she said. "I'd like to model my career on yours, I mean the way you do it all: sing, dance, act—"

"Right," Miley said, uncomfortable. She liked praise as much as the next person, but she didn't enjoy having someone gush all over her. Especially when that someone couldn't even be bothered to talk to her a couple of days ago, when she was just regular Miley from Tennessee. "Of course, it's also a lot of work."

Peyton's father approached them in time to

hear this last remark. "Oh, Peyton's a hard worker," he said. "She's willing to do whatever it takes to succeed, isn't that right, honey?"

Peyton bobbed her head. "Absolutely," she echoed. "Whatever it takes."

Her dad put her arm around her. "That's my girl," he said. "That's why Team Peyton is going to win!"

Miley's eyes met Peyton's. The other girl now looked slightly embarrassed herself. "Dad," she said softly. "I don't think you should say that in front of the judges."

"That's okay," Miley said quickly. "But speaking of which . . . I think the competition's about to start."

Mr. Fredericks turned to see the other conteststants lining up backstage. "Okay, honey, let's go get 'em!" he said as he led her away.

Joshua glanced slyly at Peyton and her father as they left, then rolled his eyes at Miley. "Civilians!" he said. "They don't have a clue about the business, do they?"

"I wouldn't call them civilians," Miley said coolly. "I'd call them fans."

He shrugged. "Whatever. So listen, about tomorrow night—"

"Sorry, no, busy busy," she said quickly. Her eyes darted around the stage, looking for an escape route, then brightened when she saw Miss Lila standing near a table and waving at them. "Oh, I think the pageant director wants us to go over to the judges' table."

"Great." He sighed heavily. "I guess we might as well get it over with." Then his mood lifted, and he smiled at Miley. "Anyway, we'll have hours to hang out together as judges, so that's cool."

She gave him a thin smile in return, but inside, she was worried. If I stay in the music business, will I turn into a jerk like this guy? One thing's for sure, if this is the price of fame, I don't want it.

Chapter Eleven

Speak your mind, but ride a fast horse.
—Traditional cowboy saying

Oliver was sitting on a wooden crate next to the chuck wagon and peeling potatoes. If he'd been asked to do this chore at home, he would have whined from the moment his mother handed him the potato peeler until the naked potatoes had been put in the pot. But now, he found that peeling potatoes could be kind of relaxing when you were doing it outdoors in the golden sunlight of late afternoon.

Plus, he was being entertained as he worked, because Dub was trying to teach Jackson how to throw a lasso, using a fence post as a target.

Oliver had learned to neatly rope the post within half an hour, then had tried to pass his newfound knowledge on to Jackson.

Unfortunately, both Jackson and Dub didn't seem to appreciate what Oliver had to offer. Dub had pronounced him a professional roper and put him on spud skinnin' duties. In the time it took him to peel seventy-three potatoes, he'd watched Jackson try and fail to rope anything, even by accident. Oliver seriously wished he had a camcorder, because the roping lesson had all the makings of an Internet classic.

"Let's go over this again, Jackson," Dub said in what he obviously imagined was a calm, patient voice. Oliver thought he sounded like a mildly annoyed grizzly bear, rather than a ferociously angry grizzly bear. "It's simple as pie! You make a loop with your rope."

Jackson nodded, his eyes intense. "Make a loop. Check."

"You shake out the kinks in the rope . . ." Dub went on.

"No more kinks." Jackson shook his rope. "Check."

"Now you step forward with your left foot and throw the rope up and over . . ."

Dub's voice trailed off in despair as Jackson whirled the loop wildly over his head, then tossed it.

"Dagnabit, boy!" Dub's former attempt at calm vanished in the blink of an eye. "You ain't got no more sense than last year's bird's nest!"

Oliver stifled a laugh.

Not only had Jackson missed the fence post, but he'd managed to rope Dub.

Dub snorted as Jackson ran over babbling apologies and untied him. When Jackson returned, red in the face, Dub yelled more instructions. "You gotta *look* at the target before you throw! And it's gotta be a smooth motion! And most of all, you gotta *commit.*"

"Right," Jackson said, breathless. "Look. Smooth motion. Commit."

As he coiled his rope and got ready to try again, Oliver saw Lizzy Lee out of the corner of his eye. She had finished grooming her horse and was now sidling up between two wagons. The girl had a deliberately casual expression on her face, as if she had just happened to wander in their direction, but Oliver saw her sneak a little peek at Jackson as he threw the lasso again.

From the sound of Dub's angry squawk, this attempt hadn't gone any better. "You call that ropin'?" he yelled. "That throw would make a dog laugh!"

"Well, at least *someone* around here'll be happy," Jackson muttered.

Oliver saw Lizzy Lee smile, and, for the first time, he started to understand what Jackson saw in her.

She was actually really cute, when she wasn't scowling and saying mean things, he thought. It was too bad she was giving Jackson such a hard time. In fact, if Oliver weren't so scared of her, he might even walk up to her and try to make Jackson's case for him. . . .

And then he found himself standing up and walking over to her before he could have second thoughts.

Once he stood in front of her, however, and faced her cool, unblinking stare, he had plenty of time for second thoughts. And third and fourth ones, for that matter.

He gulped. "Um, Lizzy Lee, I was just wondering . . ."

Oliver stopped, suddenly feeling panicky. His tongue seemed glued to the roof of his mouth. He couldn't believe he was here, he couldn't believe he was actually trying to talk to her, he couldn't believe what he was about to ask her—

"What?!" Lizzy Lee snarled. "Spit it out!"

"I was just wondering why you're being

so hard on Jackson," he said, all in a rush.

She narrowed her eyes and gave him a hard look. "Why should I tell you?"

"Well, because he's my friend," he said lamely.

He held his breath. Was she going to say something that would cut him to the core? Was she going to get mad and stomp off? Or, most likely, was she going to say something that would cut him to the core *and* stomp off?

But Lizzy Lee didn't do any of those things. Instead, she thought for a moment, then nodded. "Okay, you're right," she said.

"I am?" Oliver tried not to sound as surprised as he felt, although his voice was a little more high-pitched than usual.

"See, I met this guy at a 4-H district contest last year," Lizzy Lee began. "He was from a big city, just like your pal over there, and he was a real smooth talker. I used to have a sweet little heifer named Bluebell that I wanted to bring to the rodeo, but I had to make some money to keep raising her. I was counting on winning some top prize money at the contest, and I had a good chance, too."

Her face darkened. "But he buttered me up and got me to tell him all about what I was going to tell the judges about raising Bluebell. Then he used every point I was going to make and won the contest!"

"So what happened to Bluebell?" Oliver asked in a hushed voice.

"I had to sell her." She blinked a few times and bit her lip.

"Wow." Oliver was awed. "He done you wrong. It's just like a country song!"

Surprisingly, Lizzy Lee laughed at that. "I've never heard of a song about losing your heifer," she said. "Anyway, I've entered the calf scramble tomorrow night. Maybe I'll win a new heifer there." She glared at him. "And I'll tell you something else. I'm never trusting any city slicker ever again."

Oliver nodded slowly. "Yeah, I got it. Only . . ."

"Only what?" Telling her story seemed to have put Lizzy Lee in a better mood, somehow. She raised one mocking eyebrow, but her voice was friendlier.

"Well, just because *one* slick guy broke your heart by stealing your heifer doesn't mean they *all* will," he pointed out. "And anyway—"

Jackson whirled the rope madly over his head, lost control, and ended up with it twisted around his body. After one long moment, he tried to take a step and fell flat on his face. "Dagnabit," he murmured to the dirt. "This is a fine howdy-do."

"And anyway," Oliver said again, "Jackson's not that slick."

Lizzy Lee glanced at Jackson, who had managed to roll over and was trying to stand. He looked like a bug that had been flipped on its back and was now wiggling around, unable to turn over.

"Well," she said after a pause, "you got that right."

As Oliver ran over to help his friend get up, he thought he could hear Lizzy Lee softly laughing.

2 Chapter Twelve

Never corner something meaner than you.
—Traditional cowboy saying

"Now, here's the vegetable-judging aisle," Jim Bob said, gesturing toward an aisle lined with booths piled high with produce. "As you can see, we have competitions for best squash, zucchini, pumpkin—"

"Stop, my heart's racing as it is," Joshua said. He yawned theatrically, then smirked at Miley. "I don't think I can take all this excitement."

Miley bit her lip to keep from saying something rude. After spending hours with Joshua during the pageant interviews, she was extremely tired of his snarky comments. She would have been more than glad to skip this tour of the exhibit hall, if only to get away from him. Still, the contestants had worked hard on their homegrown vegetables and homemade pies. She and Joshua owed them some respect, some consideration, some attention—

Of course, they *had* been looking at homegrown vegetables and homemade pies for more than an hour, and Miley had to admit that her feet, in their fashionable Hannah high heels, were beginning to hurt. Her head was getting hot under her blond Hannah wig. And she felt as if she'd been flashing the same big Hannah smile for at least a century.

Before she could stop herself, she was thinking about how wonderful it would be to go back to the hotel suite and take a long, hot bath.

"Would you like to taste one of my special pickles, Hannah dear?" A woman with bright blue eyes and curly white hair fluttered over from the next booth. "I made them with a secret recipe that's been handed down in my family for generations. I'm not one to brag on myself, but I *have* won a blue ribbon fourteen years in a row."

"Wow," Joshua murmured as Miley stepped forward to take the sample the woman was holding out. "Fourteen years of prize-winning pickles. Just when I thought my day couldn't get any better—ow!"

Miley smiled sweetly at him. "Sorry."

He barely managed to turn his scowl into a smile, although it was, Miley was glad to see, a rather pained smile. "You can step on my foot any day, Hannah," he said.

"That's Joshua McAdams, isn't it?" the woman whispered to Miley. "He's mighty mannerly, isn't he? You know, my daughter just *loves* him."

Not as much as he loves himself, Miley thought.

Fortunately, she was saved from having to say anything by Lilly, who came rushing up, breathless. She was wearing a pink wig, which was slightly askew.

"Oh, hi, Lola," Miley said loudly. "Glad you could make it." Under her breath, she whispered, *"Wig."*

"What?" Lilly looked blank.

Miley tilted her head back and forth in a meaningful way.

Now Lilly was looking at her as if she were crazy.

Miley sighed. Did she have to do everything around here? "It's so good to see you!" she squealed, reaching forward to clutch Lilly's head in a playful greeting. Before Lilly could move, she jerked the wig around until it was straight.

"Ow," Lilly said, her eyes watering from having her hair pulled.

"Sorry," Miley said.

Joshua snickered. "Nobody's safe around you, are they, Hannah?"

Miley gave him a freezing look. "I *said* I was sorry."

Jim Bob checked his watch. "Okey-dokey, we're still right on schedule, but we better skedaddle over to the shopping area now or we'll be behind for the rest of the day. This way, everyone . . ."

As he hurried them past booths filled with cherry pies, apple butter, and canned okra, Joshua trailed behind, bored and making sure everyone knew it.

Fine, Miley thought. That gave her a chance to talk to Lilly, whom she hadn't seen for hours.

She glanced at Jim Bob, who was several feet ahead of them, then said under her breath, "So, *Lola*, what have you been doing all day?"

Lilly didn't meet her gaze. "Oh, you know," she said in an airy voice. "This and that."

"Uh-huh." Miley raised one eyebrow. "Is 'this and that' your code for 'hanging out with Gabe'?"

Lilly dropped her attempt to sound casual. "He is *so* cool! And he's such a good riding teacher! I've already learned how to trot and canter, and he said tomorrow he's going to teach me how to gallop! He picked out the sweetest horse for me, too. His name is Buttercup, which is a kind of a girly name for a boy horse, I know, but he's got a really sweet nature and these big brown eyes. . . ."

"Really." Miley tried to hide her smile. "I guess you like horseback riding now, huh?"

Lilly blushed. "Well, he is pretty cute."

"So you're actually interested in a country boy?" Miley asked teasingly.

"What boy?" Lilly asked innocently. "I was talking about the horse."

They were still laughing when they turned a corner and found themselves at a jewelry booth.

Miley's eyes lit up. "Oh, look, these

necklaces look like the ones we saw the other day." She picked up a turquoise pendant on a silver chain. "Hmm. You know, I still think this would go great with—"

"Excuse me," a sharp voice interrupted.

"Whoa!" Lilly's eyes widened as she recognized the woman who had yelled at Miley the day before. "It's not only the same jewelry, it's the same seller!"

But today the woman was all smiles. "Hannah Montana! I'm Tricia Louise Littleton, but you can call me Trish. It is such a pleasure to meet you!" she cried. "I am a huge, huge fan! As are millions and millions of other people, of course!"

Joshua sauntered up in time to hear this. He cleared his throat loudly. When the woman spotted him, she gave a little squeal of delight. "Oh, and Joshua McAdams! Well, if this isn't my lucky day! To have two such talented, popular singers in my booth!"

Miley bit her lip to keep from saying

something rude. Yesterday, this woman practically kicked her out of her booth! And here she was, falling all over them, just because they were celebrities! Acting as if they were royalty, just because they happened to be the tiniest bit famous! And waving her arms around and saying things like—

"Please, if you see anything you like, anything at all, it's yours," Trish said. "On the house. I would be honored if you would wear one of my pieces!"

Her eyes lit on the pendant that Miley was still holding. "That would look perfect with your blond hair!" she crowed. "Especially if you wore it with that blue jacket that you always wear for your opening song. . . ."

Miley hesitated. She knew the woman only wanted to give her the necklace because she would get publicity if Hannah Montana wore it onstage. She knew that, and she was still angry at the way she had been treated the day before, but still . . .

The necklace *was* beautiful.

She was biting her lip in indecision when she felt a sudden sharp pain in her ankle.

"Ow!" Her eyes watering, she turned her head to see Lilly giving her a meaningful look.

"Sorry," Lilly said, sounding anything but. She pulled Miley aside and said in a low voice, "Come on, this isn't why you sing, to get free stuff."

Miley stood up straighter and smiled at her friend. "You're right," she said. "Thanks."

Lilly nodded, satisfied. "Any time."

Miley lifted one eyebrow. "But I could have done without the kick in the ankle."

"Consider it payback," Lilly said, grinning. "My scalp's still all tingly."

"Hey, this jacket looks awesome!"

They turned around to see Joshua trying on a leather jacket. He caught Miley's eye and struck a pose, holding out his arms and turning around so she could get the full effect. "What do you think, Hannah?" he asked, grinning.

"Do this make me look like a real cowboy?"

"Um, yeah, Joshua, it sure does," she said. If cowboys wore jackets with appliqued flowers on the shoulders. And fringe, she added silently.

The woman in the booth looked pleased and gratified. "I'm so glad you like it."

"Like it? I love it!" Joshua said.

Miley narrowed her eyes. There was something a little too enthusiastic about Joshua's delivery, she thought. It was like he was laughing at some joke that only he understood. . . .

"In fact, it'd be great to get jackets for my backup singers, too," he went on.

The woman's smile faded a bit, but she nodded agreeably. "Well, sure, hon," she said. "I'd be pleased as punch to give you, um . . . how many jackets would that be, now?"

"Just four," he said carelessly. Then he paused, as if struck by a new thought. "Oh, but I bet my manager would love one, too! And the guy who heads up my sound crew. And my publicist . . ."

As he was speaking, he was pulling jackets off the rack.

Trish's face paled. Her smile disappeared. "Oh. Well, I was thinking more about giving *you* a jacket—" she began.

Joshua spun around. "Hey, don't worry," he said, grinning. "My boys will wear their jackets everywhere. You'll get tons of publicity."

Trish was biting her lip, but she nodded bravely. "Well, yes, I guess that's true," she said, watching him clear the racks of thousands of dollars worth of jackets. "That's . . . right nice of you."

"What a jerk!" Miley was still fuming half an hour later. Joshua had left shortly after looting Trish's booth, claiming a migraine, but looking far too gleeful for someone whose head was supposedly throbbing. Now Miley and Lilly were trailing along behind Jim Bob, letting him get far enough ahead of them so they could talk. "He totally took advantage of that woman! He knew she couldn't say no after she offered to give him a freebie."

"I'm deleting all his songs *and* his stupid video from my MP3 player as soon as I get back to the hotel," Lilly vowed. "Some people really let fame go to their heads. It's ridiculous! I mean, he's got such a sweet deal! He gets to perform all over the world, millions of people love him, he makes tons of money—he has no excuse for acting like a . . . a toad!"

Miley stopped in her tracks. "Lilly!" she said, struck by a sudden, awful thought. "I'm not a toad, am I?"

"What?" Lilly's mouth dropped open. "Are you kidding? Of course, you're not! You'd never act like Joshua, not in a million years!"

"I don't know." Miley seldom fretted, but she was fretting now. "I do love all the attention I get as Hannah, I have to admit that."

"Of course you do. Who wouldn't?" Lilly took her elbow. "Now come on, let's keep walking or we'll lose Jim Bob. And I can't wait to try some of that barbecue. . . ."

But Miley didn't move. "Wait." She glanced sideways at Lilly. "You know, I was ready to do another couple of encores at that concert last week."

"So you like to give your fans a little something extra," Lilly said, tugging a little harder on her arm.

"And it *is* really nice to stay in the presidential suite," Miley added.

"Someone's got to stay there if the president's not in town," Lilly pointed out.

"Yeah, but . . ." Miley hesitated, then said in a rush, "When that woman offered to give me that necklace, I was *this* close—" She held up her thumb and forefinger a few centimeters apart. "—to taking it! This close!"

"But you didn't," Lilly pointed out.

"Yeah," Miley nodded. "Thanks to you."

She looked serious. "You're like . . . like my little voice of conscience that keeps me from turning into another Joshua McAdams!"

"Just call me Jiminy Cricket," Lilly said.

"No, but seriously. I'm glad I have you as a friend, Lilly."

"Me, too." Lilly gave her a quick hug. "Now, come on. Let's find your dad. Maybe he'll let us sneak a spare rib."

She elbowed Miley as they started walking toward the barbecue tent. "Hey, get it? A 'spare' rib?"

"Yeah," Miley groaned. "I get it. You know what I said about how much I love our friendship? I really, really meant it." She shook her head sadly at her friend. "But, Lilly, your puns? Not so much."

Giggling, they hurried to catch up with Jim Bob.

Jim Bob took them through the barbecue tent at a forced march, giving Lilly only enough time to snag one drumstick from a preoccupied and intense Mr. Stewart. Then Miley and Lilly were ushered over to the animal exhibits, where they dutifully admired a dozen chickens, several extremely large steers, and some adorable lambs.

"I think that's about it," Jim Bob said, mopping his forehead with a handkerchief. "And right on time, too! Now we'll get you back to the hotel and—oh, wait, hold on, I almost forgot . . ."

Quickly, he steered them down another aisle. "Now, we can't let you girls go home without seeing some of Texas's prize pigs," he said. "That just wouldn't be right. And I *think*—" He checked his watch. "—yes, we just about have time if we hurry."

Miley and Lilly were practically jogging by the time they got to the end of the aisle, and Jim Bob came to a sudden halt. Breathless, they stopped, too—and Miley realized that she was standing face-to-face with Cash!

"Now, this here is Cash Garrity and his pig, Sweet Pea," Jim Bob said, reading off the sign on the stall. "Cash, I'd like to introduce Hannah Montana, one of this year's celebrity hosts for the Lone Star Rodeo, and her friend Lola Luftnagle."

Miley and Lilly exchanged wild glances. "Um . . . hi," Miley said.

"Hi," Cash said. "Nice to meet you."

There wasn't a hint of recognition in his face. Miley felt herself relax a little. This is just another meet-and-greet, she reminded herself. You've done a million of these. Just make conversation. Be nice, be charming, be witty. . . .

"That's quite a pig!" she said, then winced at how inane she sounded.

Oh, well, she thought. At least you were nice. One out of three isn't bad.

Cash smiled politely. "Oh, yeah, he's a good pig," he agreed.

There was a short, awkward silence. Cash

shuffled his feet. Miley glanced at Lilly, puzzled. It was a good thing, of course, that Cash didn't recognize her as Miley. But there was something weird going on here. . . .

"So," Cash said, clearly feeling that he had a duty to break the silence. "You're a celebrity? What is it you do?"

Miley's jaw dropped. *That's* what was weird! Cash didn't recognize her as Hannah, either!

"I sing," she said.

"Cool," Cash replied.

"Come on, are you saying you've never heard of Hannah Montana!" Lilly said, outraged on her friend's behalf. "Hello? 'The Best of Both Worlds'? 'If We Were a Movie'? 'I Got Nerve'?"

He smiled but shrugged. "Sorry. I don't listen to a lot of music. Or watch a lot of TV, even." He nodded toward Sweet Pea. "He takes up a lot of my time."

"That's okay," Miley said. "If I had a pig

like that, I'd spend a lot of time with him, too."

Lilly rolled her eyes. Miley shot her a warning look just as Jim Bob said, "Well, we've gotta be moving on. Good luck, Cash."

"Yeah," Miley said. "Good luck. Nice to meet you."

"Same here," Cash nodded. Then he turned back to scratch Sweet Pea's ears.

As they trailed along behind Jim Bob, Lilly whispered, "I can't believe it! He didn't even know who you are!"

"I know," Miley said, smiling dreamily. "Isn't that cool?"

Chapter Thirteen

It's better to keep your mouth shut and look stupid than open your mouth and prove it.

—Traditional cowboy saying

The trail riders had finally reached the rodeo arena, which meant it was time for the grand parade that would officially kick off the rodeo events, such as bronco riding and steer roping. Miley was dressed as Hannah and mounted on a frisky white horse that pranced around in front of the floats.

"Whoa," she whispered to the horse, pulling on his reins gently. "Everything's fine. Don't worry."

The horse settled down, and Miley looked

around to see if she could spot Lilly. After several minutes, she saw her with a group of other riders, behind the line of floats. Miley grinned to herself. Lilly was riding Buttercup, and Gabe was right next to her on a reddish brown horse.

Even from a distance, Lilly looked a little nervous, and Buttercup seemed to sense that. He danced sideways for a few steps, and Miley saw Lilly drop her reins and clutch the pommel of her saddle. "No, no, don't let go of your reins!" she said out loud, as if Lilly could actually hear her. "Hold on, stay in control, don't panic—"

Then Gabe reached out to grab Buttercup's reins. He rubbed his hands up and down his neck to soothe him, then said something to Lilly that made her relax and smile.

Miley relaxed a little herself. She spotted Jackson and Oliver sitting on the buckboard of the chuck wagon, lining up with the other trail riders. Oliver was chatting away to Dub, and

Jackson was craning his neck to watch that girl who had rescued him. Hmm, Miley thought. Looks like Jackson's got a little crush going. They all had a lot to catch up on now that they were back together again. . . .

Before she could pursue this line of thought any further, she heard a voice call out, "Hi, Hannah!"

She turned to see Peyton, who had just been escorted onto the lead float. Peyton wore a pale pink formal gown and long white gloves, and her hair was piled high on top of her head in an elaborate mass of curls. And she had a wide smile plastered on her face that seemed to show all of her gleaming white teeth. When she saw that she had caught Miley's attention, she raised one hand and slowly moved it back and forth in a parade wave. "You look right at home on that horse, I do declare!"

"Thanks," Miley said shortly. She didn't want Peyton, or any of the contestants, buttering her up just because she was a judge.

She clucked to her horse, intent on trotting away, but then another voice said, "So, Hannah Montana! I was hoping to run into you here."

She glanced down to see Joshua smiling flirtatiously up at her. Joshua reached out to gingerly pat her horse's nose. Her horse snorted with irritation, and Joshua snatched his hand back.

I'm with you, Miley silently told her horse. This guy would make a peacock blush.

Out loud, she said, "Well, it's in both our contracts that we ride in the opening parade, so it would be mighty strange if you didn't run into me."

"I love the way you're always kidding around," Joshua said. "You know, I really wanted to ride a horse in the parade," he added, "but my manager wouldn't let me."

"Really?" Miley's voice was cool. "My manager thought leading the Lone Star Rodeo parade was a great opportunity."

"Yeah, but you never know what might happen when animals are involved," Joshua said. As if to prove his point, Miley's horse stamped its front hoof, and Joshua jumped back in alarm. "See what I mean? What if there were a stampede or something? What if there were an accident that affected my future ability to perform?" He shook his head. "I argued with him, of course, but my manager said our insurance premiums would go through the roof."

"Yeah, that stampede clause always makes the rates go way up," Miley said drily.

Joshua smoothed down his hair, which had gotten slightly ruffled. "So, I was wondering what you had planned after the concert? Because I'd be willing to hang out for a little while. I thought I should let you know that."

Miley's horse tossed his head, almost as if he couldn't believe what Joshua was saying, either. She had to bite her lip to keep from laughing. "Thanks," she said, "but I'm usually pretty tired after a show. I'll probably just go back to the hotel."

"You sure?" Joshua fixed his bright blue gaze—the gaze that *Entertainment Insider* had called "a laser beam of cobalt blue"—on her face. He lowered his voice and gave her a deep and meaningful look. "'Cause, you know, I always thought that if *we* were a movie, we'd be the kind that wins Oscars."

More like the kind that goes straight to DVD, Miley thought. It was hard to tell for sure, but she could have sworn that her horse was rolling his eyes.

"Another time, maybe," she said, hoping that the parade would start soon.

Fortunately, she was saved by a girl on the parade float calling out flirtatiously, "Hey, Joshua, what are you doing down there?"

"Yeah, you should be on the float with us!" another girl added.

This was greeted by a chorus of giggles

from half a dozen other beauty pageant contestants who had now joined Peyton on the lead float.

Joshua looked up at Miley. "Duty calls." He smirked.

Miley shook her head as she watched him go, then she gathered up the reins and got ready for the parade to start.

"Ladies and gentlemen, welcome to the Lone Star Rodeo!" a voice boomed out from the PA system. The audience cheered. "And please give a big Texas howdy to the grand marshal of this year's parade, Miss Hannah Montana!"

The cheering turned into full-throttle screaming. As Miley rode her horse into the arena, her heart pounding with excitement, she felt completely happy . . . and right at home.

Two hours later, she was sitting next to Joshua at the judges' table and wishing that she could be anywhere else. Siberia in winter, a desert island with no MP3 player, a swamp filled with quicksand and crocodiles . . . anything would be better than sitting through the talent portion of this particular beauty pageant.

So far, the competition had consisted of a tap dance that was so spirited it ended in a sprained ankle, a screeching version of the national anthem, a dramatic monologue loosely based on the discovery of the south pole, and incredibly enough, a ventriloquist act. Miley's head ached from the effort of looking bright, interested, and encouraging, and Joshua's constant whispered commentary wasn't helping.

As a thin, nervous girl with glasses finished her dance recital with a wobbly pirouette that clearly left her dizzy, Joshua leaned over to whisper in Miley's ear. "Yet another argument in support of leaving performing to the professionals."

"I thought she did fine, considering," Miley said, irritated.

"Considering that she didn't actually fall off the stage?" he said. "If that's the criteria you're using as a judge, we have a long night ahead of us."

"Shh!" Miley gestured toward the stage, where the emcee was about to announce the next entry. "It's time for the next contestant."

"Oh, yay," Joshua murmured sarcastically. "I can hardly wait to see what kind of talent this one has dredged up."

The emcee looked down at an index card, then said into the microphone, "Please welcome Sarah Jane Williams, Miss South Dakota, who will be portraying Lady Macbeth . . . in mime."

Miley's eyes widened in dismay, but she kept smiling until she felt like a pageant contestant herself.

☆   ☆   ☆

After five more entries, Peyton took the stage. Miley crossed her fingers under the table. As much as she didn't like the new Peyton, she still remembered the old Angela with fondness. It would be so great if Peyton knocked their socks off and won the talent competition, maybe even the whole pageant. . . .

Then Peyton opened her mouth to sing, and Miley's heart sank.

It wasn't that Peyton was *bad*. She sang in tune, and she had good stage presence. But she had chosen a power ballad, and she was belting it out with such force that her voice was strained with the effort. Clearly, this wasn't her natural style.

Miley caught a brief glimpse of Peyton's dad standing backstage. He was grinning broadly as Peyton kept singing at the top of her lungs. Finally, mercifully, the song ended. Peyton took her bow and left the stage.

"And that, ladies and gentlemen, is the end of the talent competition," the emcee announced. "Please remain in your seats. We'll have a brief intermission, then the girls will walk the stage for the evening gown competition. Our judges will deliver their verdict, and your Lone Star Rodeo queen will be announced!"

"So, Hannah, do you want to compare notes?" Joshua held up his legal pad on which he had scrawled "NO!" next to every contestant's name. "Or should we just pull a name out of a hat?"

"We're judges, we need to judge," Miley said. "But first, I need to go, um, fix my makeup." And get as far away from you as possible for as long as possible, she thought.

With a sense of relief, she hurried to the dressing rooms backstage. But Miley wanted a place to be alone for a few minutes, and the dressing rooms were a beehive of activity, with girls changing clothes, redoing their makeup, fixing their hair, and chattering excitedly about how they had done. So she quickly backed out and started wandering around the backstage area, which was filled with props and old sets. Finally, she found a quiet spot where she could sit by herself, take a few deep breaths, and meditate on that shining moment, somewhere in the future, when she would no longer have to see, hear, or deal with Joshua McAdams in any way.

She had just achieved the perfect state of calm relaxation when the silence was broken by the sound of a tune being picked out on a piano. Miley frowned at this interruption—then her expression changed to surprise and finally to interest as a girl began singing along.

Whoever she was, she was more talented than anyone they had just seen onstage, Miley thought. The girl's voice was a little rough, but her pitch and tone were true. And there was something else, something that had caught Miley's ear and made her keep listening. . . .

Miley tilted her head slowly to one side, considering. Yes . . . what was even more impressive was that this voice didn't sound like anyone else. Whoever the girl was, she sounded original. Unique. Her own person, and no one else.

Miley stood up and quietly edged her way around the sets until she saw an upright piano wedged in between a styrofoam cow statue and the set for an Old West jail cell. The girl sitting at the piano was Peyton. She had changed into her evening gown, but her high heels were lying on the floor where she had kicked them off.

As Miley stopped in surprise, she accidentally bumped into a chair, which skittered across the floor. Peyton abruptly stopped singing and turned to face her.

"Oh, hi." Peyton's voice was flat. This was not at all the kind of greeting she usually gave to Hannah Montana. "I didn't know anyone else was back here."

"Neither did I," Miley said. "I was just looking for a quiet place to be alone for a few minutes."

"I'm sorry, I'll leave," Peyton began.

"No, no, I'm sorry to interrupt," Miley said. "What you were singing just now . . . that was beautiful."

"Really?" Peyton asked shyly. "I was just fooling around."

"Well, you sounded great," Miley said. "You should sing that way all the time."

"You mean instead of singing the way I just did onstage?" Peyton smiled ruefully at Miley's expression. "You don't need to look so surprised. I know I sound horrible when I perform that way."

"Then why do it?" Miley asked. "If it doesn't feel natural—"

Peyton's face became a mask. "Because that's the kind of performance that gets you crowned beauty queen," she said. "At least according to Team Peyton."

"Listen, Peyton," Miley began, then she stopped.

"What?" The other girl gave her a long look. "Come on, you were going to say something. Go ahead. You won't hurt my feelings." She shrugged. "I know I'm not going to win this beauty pageant."

"No, you're not," Miley agreed. "But see, the thing is . . . I don't think you care that much whether you win."

Peyton's mask dropped. "Why do you say that?"

Miley took a deep breath and decided to opt for honesty. "Because you don't look comfortable out there," Miley said. "You seem to be trying too hard. Winning pageants isn't because of what you call yourself or the dress your designer picks out for you. You have to be true to who you really are, and people can sense when you're not."

Peyton met Miley's eyes as she took that in. Finally, she nodded. "You're right," she said softly. "But my dad's put so much work into this and spent so much money. He really wants me to be famous at something. Singing, acting, it doesn't really matter. Just . . . famous." She lifted her chin slightly. "Like you."

"None of that matters if it's not what *you* want." Miley paused to choose her words carefully. "Here's the thing: I really do love performing. And the way I sing, it's the way that's always come naturally to me. The way you were singing, just now"—Miley nodded toward the piano—"that was your real voice, I think."

"Yeah." Peyton sounded wistful.

"And my life onstage," Miley went on. "That's only part of who I am. I'd never want to get so famous that I forgot who I was or what was important to me, like my friends and family. All I'm saying is . . . live your own dream. Nobody else's."

For a few seconds, Peyton didn't say a

word. Then her father came rushing over, looking annoyed.

"Peyton! Why in the world are you over here?" he shouted. "Get your shoes on! It's time for you to go onstage. I'll go tell the emcee you're on your way. Now hurry!"

"I'll be right there, Daddy," she said as he rushed off. She stood up from the piano bench, slipped on her shoes, and threw her shoulders back. In an instant, she transformed herself into the picture of self-confidence.

"I guess it's time for me to get back to the judging table, too," Miley said.

Peyton gave Miley a brilliant smile, but her eyes were distant. "Thanks for the advice," she said politely.

Then Peyton made her way to the wings, nodded to the emcee, and strode out onto the stage.

Miley knew she should rejoin Joshua, but she stood still for a moment longer, watching as Peyton walked regally into the spotlight.

She looked dazzling, Miley thought, like a real beauty queen. She just hoped that Peyton would eventually figure out a way to dazzle on her own and find her own spotlight.

⇜⇝ Chapter Fourteen

*If you're ridin' ahead of the herd, take a look back
every now and then to make sure it's still there with ya.*
—Traditional cowboy saying

"I can't wait to see the steer roping." Oliver
stood on his toes, peering out the window of the
private box that had been set aside for the use of
Hannah Montana and her entourage. "Did I tell
you that Dub used to rope steers? He says it's
the hardest sport at the rodeo. He says only the
bravest and most talented cowboys can do it. He
says—"

"Enough already with The World According
to Dub!" Miley said. The concert didn't start
until after the evening's rodeo events, and

Joshua was the opening act, so she had at least three hours before she went onstage, but she was already dressed as Hannah Montana. "Ever since you got back from the trail ride, the only thing you can talk about is that Dub."

"Hey, what can I say?" Oliver said. "He's a cool dude."

He wandered over to the buffet table, where Mr. Stewart, dressed in his manager disguise, was examining the spread.

Oliver's face brightened as he lifted the silver cover off one of the dishes. "Ooh, minicheeseburgers!" he said, grabbing one and eating it in two bites. "I was thinking maybe I should become a cowboy after college," he said after swallowing. "Did I tell you what Dub said? He said I'm a natural at the cowboy life. And you know what else he said?"

Before he could go on, the door opened and Lilly dashed in. She was wearing her red Lola wig, a green minidress, red-and-white-striped knee-high socks, and sneakers. "Hey, sorry

I'm late," she said breathlessly. "Wasn't the parade fun? Gabe showed me how to groom Buttercup and then we got to talking—and do you know what he said? He said I looked like I was born riding a horse! He said I could come back to Texas anytime for more lessons!"

"Well, you two sure are singin' a different tune than you were back in Malibu," Mr. Stewart said.

Lilly and Oliver gave him a puzzled look.

"You know, last week, when you both swore you hated horses and wouldn't ride one if you were hog-tied to the saddle?" he reminded them.

"Hate horses?" Lilly sounded as if she didn't know what Mr. Stewart was talking about. "Us?"

"Impossible," Oliver said, shocked. "They're the noblest of beasts!"

"I never thought I'd see the day when you two went country." He chuckled. "The only thing stranger than that would be if Jackson decided to turn country. Speaking of which . . . Where is that boy, anyway? He said something about a surprise. . . ."

Miley and Lilly shrugged, but Oliver got a pleased, secretive look on his face.

Just then, the lights dimmed, and a voice boomed out over the stadium's PA system. "Welcome, ladies and gentlemen, to the opening night of the Lone Star Rodeo!"

A spotlight hit a girl standing on a horse and holding a huge American flag. She was wearing a white cowboy hat and a sequined red-white-and-blue jumpsuit. As the national anthem played, she raced her horse around the ring, the flag waving behind her. As she made her last circuit and rode the horse out of the arena, fireworks burst over the stadium's open ceiling. The crowd whistled and cheered.

"Wow," Miley said. "Now *that's* the way to open a show!" Her eyes lit up. "Daddy! I just had a great idea! Why don't we start my concert with *fireworks*—"

"No," Mr. Stewart said firmly. "Now don't distract me with ideas like that, not when I'm waiting for Jackson's surprise. I'm nervous enough as it is."

"Before we get to the steer ropin' and the bronco bustin', we're going to start with everyone's favorite event," the announcer went on. "The calf scramble!"

The audience went wild, but inside Hannah Montana's private box, everyone just looked at one another, confused.

"Calf scramble?" Lilly asked. "What's that?"

"Dub told me all about it," Oliver said. He glanced at Miley. "Too bad I can't pass that information on. Too bad I've been forbidden to reference my good friend Dub, even though he has taught me so much. Like what a calf scramble is."

"Oliver, for heaven's sake—" Miley began.

She was interrupted by the sound of the announcer reading off the list of participants . . . and he called out Jackson's name!

Now they were more than confused. They were completely befuddled—everyone except Oliver, that is.

"Jackson's competing in the rodeo?" Mr. Stewart pressed his nose against the glass. "What in tarnation is he doing?"

"I could tell you that," Oliver said. "Except that this plan was cooked up by me and Dub, to help Jackson out." He sighed, obviously trying not to look too pleased with himself. "If only I could talk about Dub . . . but no. I've been forced to take a vow of silence—"

"I'm going to force you to take a vow of everlasting pain if you don't tell us what's going on, right now!" Miley said.

Oliver grinned. "It's simple," he said. "And brilliant, if I do say so myself. See, the rodeo lets a bunch of heifers loose in the arena. All the competitors try to catch one. And if you catch it, you keep it."

Stunned, they turned to look down at the arena, where the calves had just been let loose. They began running every which way, throwing up little clouds of dust, as dozens of teenagers began chasing them. Even from a distance, they could see Jackson running wildly.

He'd lunge for a heifer's head, miss, and land face down in the dirt.

He'd grab a tail and get dragged for several yards before losing his grip.

Once, he managed to wrestle a calf to the ground, only to have it step on his stomach and jerk free.

"Come on, Jackson!" Lilly started cheering him on. "You can do it!"

"Hold him around the neck!" Oliver urged.

"Hold on tight!" Miley yelled. She grinned at her dad. "I guess Jackson's finally getting into the rodeo spirit!" she said. "Oh, look, he almost caught that little brown one!"

From the private box high above the arena, Mr. Stewart stared down at his son in dismay. "Jackson's sure showing gumption, I have to give him that," he said. "But what in the world are we gonna do with a cow back in California?"

Time was running out for Jackson. He had only three minutes left to grab a calf, get a halter over its head, and maneveur it inside the square that had been marked out on the arena floor. If he lost this chance, he knew he'd lose Lizzy Lee forever.

Sweat dripped off the end of his nose and ran into his eyes, making them sting and blur. He took a deep breath and blinked several times in order to focus his gaze . . . and that's when he saw the most beautiful sight he'd ever laid eyes on—a brown calf with a white patch over one eye. Even better, she had a sweet expression, as if she wouldn't dream of running away, slipping out of his arms or stepping on his foot. Best of all, she was standing absolutely still, only a yard away from him.

"Hold still there," he said softly as he began edging toward her, the halter dangling from his hand.

There was chaos all around him as other kids chased their own calves, yelling and waving their arms in an attempt to herd the animals in the right direction. For their part, the calves were running away, eluding capture with sudden changes of direction, and bawling at the top of their lungs. There was a distant, constant roar of yelling and cheering from the stands.

But for Jackson, the world had dwindled until it contained just him and that brown calf with the white spot.

"Come on, now, you look like you believe in true love," he murmured.

The calf blinked at him. Maybe she was a little tired and that's why she wasn't running away, he thought as he took a few more cautious steps in her direction. Almost within reach now . . .

Or maybe . . . maybe she had sensed, with her animal intuition, what was at stake for him! Maybe she was actually on his side! Jackson decided to test this theory out.

"You don't want to see me get my heart broken, do you?" He stretched out a hand, coaxing, beseeching the calf to step closer. "You're a champion of true love, aren't you?"

Just one more step . . .

And then the calf bolted!

"Aaaggghhh!" Jackson yelled, giving chase.

"One minute left!" the announcer called out.

The calf glanced over her shoulder as he raced, red-faced, after her. Jackson could have sworn she was laughing at him.

And that was just the spur he needed. He put on an extra burst of speed and flung himself forward as the calf darted past the corner of the winner's square.

"Gotcha!" he yelled into the calf's ear. Then

213

he fell backward into the square. The calf landed on top of him just as the final buzzer went off.

"Good job, son!" The announcer called out. "You made it into the winner's square with one second to go! You just won yourself a nice little heifer!"

But the wind had been knocked out of Jackson. All he could do was smile weakly . . . and hope that somebody would come over and lift the calf off him. *Soon.*

"Congratulations." Lizzy Lee stood over Jackson, holding out her hand. His calf had gotten to her feet on her own, so Jackson took Lizzy Lee's hand and let her pull him up.

"That was a right good job you did," she added, handing him the calf's halter.

"Thanks," he said. His voice sounded a little wheezy, but at least he could talk. "How'd you do?"

"Came up empty this time." She tried to

shrug as if it didn't matter. "Can't say I didn't try my hardest, though."

Jackson looked her over. Her shirttail was pulled out of her jeans. Most of her hair had come out of her ponytail and was straggling down her back. Her face was grimy, and every inch of her clothing was covered in dirt. "I guess the calf just tried harder," he said.

Lizzy Lee grinned slightly. "That's one way to look at it." She looked down, scuffing the toe of her boot in the ground. "Oh, well. There's always next year."

"Actually . . ." Jackson hesitated. This was it, the culmination of the cunning plan that he and Oliver had cooked up last night. But unlike most of his schemes, which Jackson usually had complete confidence would succeed, this one suddenly felt a little shaky.

Jackson did not like this feeling. He did not like it at all. He cleared his throat and tried again. "That is, um, I was going to say . . ."

His voice trailed off once more. Suddenly,

in a blinding flash of insight, he knew exactly what his problem was. It was Lizzy Lee! He'd never met anyone like her, so he had no idea how she would respond to what he was about to say. And whether he met with success or failure in the next few seconds depended entirely on her reaction.

She gave him an amused look. "Speak up, cowboy," she said, a note of her usual sarcasm back in her voice. "I can't seem to hear you."

"I just wanted to say that I won this calf for you!" he blurted out.

"What?" Lizzy Lee's mouth dropped open.

"Oliver told me how you lost your other heifer, so I decided to get you another one," he said. "Here."

He handed her the lead rope.

She looked down at it, then back up at him. "Is this your idea of sweet talk, city boy?" she asked, smiling slightly.

"Yeah," Jackson said. "I figured it'd work better than flowers."

Her smile grew a little wider. "You got that right."

Jackson's heart gave a leap. His plan had worked! Now it was time to ask the most important question of all. . . .

As they walked out of the arena, the calf trailing behind them, he said, "So, do you want to watch the Hannah Montana concert with me?"

Lizzy Lee gave him a sideways glance. "I don't care if I do," she said.

"Great!" Jackson said. Three steps later, he asked, "That *was* a yes, right?"

For the first time since he'd met her, Lizzy Lee laughed. "Yes," she said. "That was a yes."

A few hours later, Jackson and Lizzy Lee were sitting in the highest seats in the stadium, looking down at the stage far, far below them.

"Thanks for using my tickets instead of hanging out in that fancy private box," Lizzy Lee said. "The seats aren't that great, but—"

"They're perfect," he said quickly. And private, he thought gleefully.

Lizzy Lee squinted at the stage. "But the view's not nearly as good," she went on. "That Hannah Montana looks like an ant from up here."

"That's okay," Jackson said. "Believe me, I see enough of her as it is."

They listened as Hannah sang a song. They tapped their toes as she danced across the stage. They bobbed their heads and sang along now and then. And the whole time, Jackson was debating with himself. Exactly how friendly should he try to get with Lizzy Lee? True, she'd agreed to sit with him for the concert. On the other hand, Lizzy Lee was . . . Lizzy Lee. Jackson sure didn't want to guess wrong when it came to a girl who could throw him to the ground and hog-tie him if she got mad.

He worried about this dilemma for three more songs. Then Hannah Montana told her audience that she was going to take a short break.

For a few moments, Jackson and Lizzy Lee sat in silence. Then she turned her head slightly and said, "You know, you can put your arm around me. If you want to."

Jackson froze.

He glanced at her out of the corner of his eye and was amazed to see that Lizzy Lee was . . . actually blushing!

"I mean," she added shyly, "if you want to."

He waited for a few seconds, until his heart slowed down. Then he let his breath out and said, as casually as possible, "I don't care if I do."

$\mathscr{Q}\mathord{\supset}$ Chapter Fifteen

Go after life as if it's something that's got to be roped in a hurry before it gets away.

—Traditional cowboy saying

After finishing her concert, Miley did a fast change out of her Hannah Montana costume, then raced through the crowd on the midway, looking for Lilly. When she spotted her standing by the Ferris wheel with Cash and Gabe, she rushed over.

"Hey, y'all," she said. "So, where's Oliver? And what ride should we go on first . . . or do you want to get something to eat now and then go on rides—"

"Not so fast," a voice said behind her.

Miley turned around to see her dad standing there with Oliver. Mr. Stewart was holding a huge trophy.

"Dad!" she said. "You did it! You won the Golden Brisket!"

"With a little help from my sweet Bessie, of course," he said happily. Then he spied Cash and Gabe. "Do I know you boys?"

"Oh, sorry, Daddy," Miley said. She quickly introduced them, adding, "And Bessie, of course, is his barbecue grill."

She held her breath, waiting for Cash and Gabe to make fun of this. But, somewhat to her surprise, they both nodded seriously, as if naming a grill made total sense.

"She must be a beaut for you to win the Golden Brisket," Cash said. "That's a tough competition."

"Yeah, my uncle's entered it for years, and he never gets past the semis," Gabe added. "Congratulations."

"Thanks, boys," Mr. Stewart said. He lifted

the trophy above his head. "I'm the king of the barbecue world!" He held the pose for several seconds, then muttered out of the corner of his mouth, "Oliver! Photo op!"

Oliver jumped up obediently and snapped several shots of Mr. Stewart holding up his trophy.

"Got it!" he said. He checked the display on the back of his digital camera. "But my memory's kind of low now. I mean, I already have more than two hundred shots of you and the Golden Brisket, Mr. Stewart. I think that's enough."

"Fine," Mr. Stewart said, giving his trophy one last, fond polish. "As long as my moment of triumph is well-documented."

"Oh, it is," Oliver assured him. "Believe me. Even the last presidential inauguration didn't get this much coverage."

"And that's exactly as it should be," Mr. Stewart said with a self-satisfied nod. "Now, if you young'uns will excuse me, I think I'll take my trophy for a little stroll. And if there happen to be some paparazzi around who are desperate to get a shot of this year's barbecue champion, well, this'll be their lucky night."

"Great idea, Dad," Miley said. "Call me on my cell if the media frenzy gets out of control."

"Will do, bud," he said with a wink. "Y'all have fun, now."

As he strolled off, Miley looked at her friends. "Okay," she said. "What ride should we go on first?"

"I vote for Thunder Rocket," Lilly said. "It goes so fast, your blood reverses direction!"

"Huh," Miley said faintly. "Sounds like fun."

"I vote for the Vomit Comet," Oliver said. "Fifty-two percent of the people who ride it throw up before it's over."

"Right," Miley said, turning green.

Cash caught her eye and winked. She

smiled back. He seemed to know just how she was feeling, because he said smoothly, "Well, those rides do sound real fun . . . but how about we start with the Ferris wheel? I hear the view of the fairgrounds is great when you get to the top."

They ended up buying snacks to eat while they kept debating which ride to try first. Lilly and Oliver sat down on a bench to share a tub of popcorn, while Miley ran over to a concession stand to buy sodas.

As she was standing in line, she heard someone call out, "Hey, Miley!" and turned to see a girl with long black hair standing a few feet away.

At first, Miley didn't recognize her. Then she did a double-take. "Peyton?"

"Actually," Peyton said, sounding a little embarrassed, "I've gone back to Angela." She was wearing jeans, a plain T-shirt, and old cowboy boots. Her hair was pulled back in a simple ponytail, and her only makeup was lip gloss and a little mascara.

"You look great," Miley said sincerely. "But, um . . ."

"What happened to Peyton?" Angela finished. She laughed. "I don't know, and, honestly, I don't care."

"I'm sorry you didn't win the pageant," Miley said.

Peyton shrugged. "That's okay. It turns out that I learned a lot anyway." She smiled mischieviously. "Unfortunately, they weren't the lessons my pageant coach wanted me to learn!"

"Oh, really?" Out of the corner of her eye, Miley could see Lilly, Oliver, Cash, and Gabe waiting for her. But she was too curious about Peyton's sudden change of heart to rush back to them. "So, what did you learn? If you don't mind my asking?"

The corner of Angela's mouth lifted. "Actually, it was something Hannah Montana said to me," she said. Her voice sounded shy. She added hurriedly, "I hope you don't think I'm name dropping—"

"No, no, not at all," Miley reassured her, her curiosity amped up even further. "What did she say?"

"To live my own dream." Angela shrugged. "I know it sounds obvious, but—well, it really hit home. Maybe it was the way she said it."

Miley smiled at her. "Sounds like you were ready to hear it, too."

"More than ready," Angela said, laughing. "I just didn't know it."

"Hey, Angela!" They turned to see two of the other beauty pageant contestants waving. "We got tickets for the fun house! Come on!"

"Be right there!" Angela said. She turned back to Miley. "Hey, if you're going to be around tomorrow, maybe we could have some lunch or something? And talk about the old days in Crowley Corners?"

"Sounds great," Miley said warmly. "I'll see you around, Angela."

When they got to the Ferris wheel, all of them squeezed into one car and sat in seats facing each other. As the wheel turned and they rose up toward the starry night sky, Miley was quiet, listening to the others laugh and joke.

When their car reached the top, the wheel stopped for a moment and everyone looked out at the flashing lights of the midway below . . . everyone except Miley. She looked at the smiling faces of Lilly and Oliver, her old friends, and Cash and Gabe, her new friends, and thought about how lucky she was.

Lucky to be Hannah Montana, famous pop star.

And even luckier to be Miley Stewart, a girl with the best friends and family in the world.

Acknowledgments

Thanks to Renee Sanders, Rachael Sanders, Lynn Vasquez, Jennifer Fletcher, and Paula Tafelski for a great time at the rodeo, and, of course, a special shout-out to Liz Rudnick, editor extraordinaire!

About the Author

Suzanne Harper has written two novels for teens, *The Secret Life of Sparrow Delaney* and *The Juliet Club*, as well as several nonfiction books, numerous magazine articles, and several plays. She earned degrees in English and journalism from the University of Texas at Austin and a master's degree in writing from the University of Southern California. She lives in New York City. You can visit her at her Web site, www.suzanneharper.com.

Check out the first original story!

ROCK THE WAVES

by Suzanne Harper

Based on the series created by Michael Poryes and Rich Correll & Barry O'Brien

Ride the wave
Summer sun, summer fun, summer love
Ride the wave
Let it bring you what you're dreaming of

The sun had already risen high in the cloudless blue sky over Malibu by the time fifteen-year-old Miley Stewart woke up. She pushed a strand of brown hair out of her eyes and blinked sleepily at her bedroom ceiling, sensing that there was something different—something delightful—about this morning. The only problem was that she couldn't quite remember what it was.

Two birds sang sweetly to each other in the jacaranda tree outside. She turned her head toward the window, smiling, then realized that this was the first thing that was different: she could actually *hear* the birds. Usually, the gentle sound of birdsong would be totally drowned out by the painful sound of her older brother, Jackson, singing loudly and incredibly off-key in the bathroom.

She lay still for another moment, luxuriating in the sense of peace and watching dust motes dance lazily in the sunlight that slanted through the window curtains.

Then she stretched her arms over her head, enjoying the feeling of being completely rested and relaxed . . . which, now that she thought about it, was also strange. Usually, every morning started with her desperately trying to find the braying alarm clock so she could hit the snooze button one more time. . . .

That was it! Her alarm clock hadn't gone off! Miley bolted out of bed, panicky, and raced to her closet. She should have known as soon as she saw the way the sunbeams crossed her room that the sun was higher in the sky than usual, which meant that it was very late, which meant that she would probably miss the first bell, which meant . . .

She stopped abruptly in the middle of the room as she finally remembered the glorious fact that had been nagging at her since she first woke up.

No, she wasn't going to be tardy. Because *this* was the first day of summer! Three months of fun and friends and freedom stretched out in front of her, like a glorious present waiting to be unwrapped!

Miley did a little dance of joy before running out of her room and down the stairs.

"Good morning!" she called out to her father, who was mixing pancake batter in the kitchen.

"Well, someone's in a good mood today," Robby Ray Stewart said teasingly. "Hmm. I wonder why that is?"

"Because I'm free," she said happily. "Free, free, free!"

Miley skidded to a stop and reached over the counter to put a finger in the bowl of batter. "Free," she repeated dreamily one more time as she licked her finger.

"Whoa, there, bud, you can lick the bowl *after* I've finished making pancakes for everybody," her father said.

"But there won't *be* any batter left after you've made the pancakes," Miley pointed out reasonably. She snuck her finger in the bowl again. "Yum."

"Mornin'," Jackson said, wandering into the kitchen. His tousled dark blond hair made it clear he'd just stumbled out of bed. So did the fact that he was still wearing pajama bottoms and a T-shirt. Yawning, he grabbed a plate and held it out to his dad. "The pancakes smell great. I'll have five, please. No, seven. Actually, I'm starving, so how about eight. . . ?"

"Whoa, whoa, whoa," Mr. Stewart said. "Don't you want to take a gander at my works of art here first?"

Miley rolled her eyes. Her father had grown very proud of his ability to create what he called "picture pancakes"—batter poured to resemble objects and animals—and insisted on asking his children to identify them before being served.

Unfortunately, trying to figure out what the pancakes were supposed to be wasn't always that easy. Mr. Stewart would claim that the pancakes were alien spacecraft or giraffes or pickup trucks, but they all looked like blobs to Miley. Tasty blobs, but blobs nonetheless.

Jackson peered suspiciously at the skillet. "Oh, man. Is that a tarantula? You know I hate eating anything that looks like a spider."

"Now, why in tarnation would I make a tarantula pancake?" his father asked testily. "Look closer."

Jackson tried again. "An octopus?"

"No! Open your eyes, boy!"

Jackson's stomach growled. His hunger drove him to start making wild guesses. "An amoeba? A sailing ship? A car engine?"

"No, no, and no." His father flipped the pancake, looking hurt. "It's a palm tree! I can't believe you couldn't see that!"

"Oh, yeah, *now* I do," Jackson said, hoping to get back in his dad's good graces—and get some breakfast—as soon as possible. "I must not be awake yet! Or maybe that gnawing hunger in my stomach is making me so light-headed that I can't think properly." With a hopeful expression, he held out his plate.

"Nice try," Mr. Stewart said grumpily, but he slid a few pancakes onto his son's plate. As he was adding a touch of nutmeg to the batter, the back door opened and Lilly Truscott, Miley's best friend, burst into the room carrying a Boogie board. She was wearing a T-shirt and shorts over a bathing suit, and her blond hair was braided in a no-nonsense way that meant she was ready for action. "Hey, everybody! Happy first day of summer vacation!"

She traded a high five with Miley, then sniffed the air. "Wow, something sure smells delicious."

Mr. Stewart beamed as he carefully poured more batter into the skillet. "That would be my world-famous pancakes," he said, bragging. "Come on, Lilly. Check out this one."

Lilly gave Miley a long-suffering look; she had been subjected to picture pancakes on several occasions when she had slept over at the Stewarts' house.

"Daddy, just let us eat breakfast!" Miley

cried. "We're so hungry!"

"In a second, bud," he said. "Take a gander at this skillet, Lilly. You're usually good at this."

Reluctantly, Lilly went over to the stove. "Um, is it, maybe, a . . . snowman?"

"A snowman?" Mr. Stewart asked, outraged. "Snowmen are for amateurs. I moved past snowmen years ago!"

"A rose garden? A map of the United States? A line of ducks walking through a puddle?" Under pressure, Lilly was beginning to babble as much as Jackson had.

Exasperated, Mr. Stewart held out the skillet to the room and pointed at the pancake with his spatula. "It's Mount Rushmore!" he said, as if this were blindingly obvious. "Can't you see how I used extra cinnamon on Lincoln's beard?"

Miley, Lilly, and Jackson stared at the pancake doubtfully.

"Come on," Mr. Stewart said. "Just squint

your left eye and tilt your head to the right, and you'll see it plain as the nose on your face."

"Oh. Yeah. Of course," Miley said, trying not to laugh. "I *can't* believe I didn't see that from the beginning."

"I think I need to take you kids to the eye doctor," her father said grumpily as he started a new batch of pancakes. "You're developing serious vision problems."

The door opened again and Oliver Oken, Miley's other best friend, bounded into the kitchen, smiling. *"Hola!"* he cried. He had started taking Spanish and liked to use his newfound vocabulary whenever possible. *"Cómo estás?"*

"Hey, Oliver," Miley said. *"Bueno."*

"Hi, Miley," he said. "Morning, Mr. Stewart." He peered into the pan, brushing his brown bangs out of his eyes so that he could get a better look. "That's an airplane, isn't it?" he asked. "A 747 jumbo jet, if I'm not mistaken?"

Mr. Stewart brightened immediately. "Got

it first time out of the chute!" he cried before turning an accusing glare on the others. "See what happens when people take artistic creation seriously?" He turned back to Oliver. "You feel like breakfast, Oliver?"

"You bet." Oliver's brown eyes lit up. True, he had just finished eating two bowls of cereal and four pieces of toast, but he reasoned that he needed extra nutrition because he was still growing. At least, he *hoped* he was still growing.

"Then grab a seat." Mr. Stewart put a stack of pancakes on the breakfast table. "And get to eatin', everybody. The pancakes may be pretty as a picture, but they aren't any good when they're cold."

"Thanks!" Oliver speared a few pancakes, poured on some syrup, and dug in. "So, Miley, what's so important we had to get up at the crack of dawn on our very first day of summer vacation?"

"*That's* what's important," she said. "Vacation! I counted up last night. We only have one hundred days of freedom! We have to make the most of it. So I have called you here today for a summer-strategy session."

"You sound like you're running for president," Jackson mumbled through a big bite of pancake.

"And you sound like you're talking with your mouth full," she snapped back.

"Hey, be sweet, you two," their father said. "No fussin' or feudin' over the flapjacks! Especially not flapjacks like these—flapjacks that belong in a museum." He took one last appreciative look at his own plate. "That's Elvis," he said, pointing to his breakfast before taking a bite.

"First," Miley went on, thinking out loud, "we have to be sure to block out mornings at the beach."

"Absolutely. That's a given," Lilly said. She gave her friend an encouraging look. "Maybe this will be the summer you'll finally let me teach you how to surf."

But Miley shook her head. "No way," she said with finality. "You *know* I'd be taking my life in my hands."

Lilly was a total athlete. She loved skateboarding, surfing, running, playing basketball. But even though Miley had grown up riding horses on a farm in Tennessee, she was a major klutz when it came to most sports. She was always the last one picked for the team in gym class and the first one to drop a ball or twist an ankle. The thought of trying to balance on a surfboard while also braving the crashing waves of Malibu made her break out in a nervous sweat. So, as much as Lilly begged her to give surfing a go, Miley had always managed to resist.

"You'd love it if you just gave it a try," Lilly wheedled. "And we'd have even more time to hang out once you learned. Just think about it."

"Okay." Miley put her finger to her chin and frowned to demonstrate how hard she was thinking. Then she shook her head again. "The answer's still no."

Lilly sighed. "Well, at least we can hang out at the park. They've got a sweet new half-pipe."

Miley had silently resolved never to try skateboarding, either, but she decided this was not the best time to mention that. Instead, she tried a diversionary tactic. "We also have to make time for shopping," she said.

Her tactic worked. Lilly's face brightened. Here was an activity they could both whole-heartedly enjoy. "Summer sales at the mall are a must," she agreed.

Oliver looked up from his pancakes in alarm. Once shopping entered the summer-planning discussion, he knew it was time to make his opinion heard. "Don't forget going to the movies," he said. "'Tis the season of summer blockbusters!"

"Yeah," Miley said. "See what I mean? There's so much to do!" Her eyes narrowed in thought. "Maybe we should try and make a schedule—"

"Whoa, bud, slow down there!" Mr.

Stewart said. "I hate to be the one to break it to you, Miley, but this summer isn't going to be all fun and games."

"It isn't?" Miley eyed her dad warily. "Why not?"

He eyed her back. "Well, I've got some good news and some bad news. Which do you want first?"

Miley bit her lip. She hated these kinds of choices; they made her feel as if her life had become a game show and she had just entered the crucial final round and was about to give a completely wrong answer.

When she hesitated, Oliver jumped in with his advice. "Ask for the bad news first. That way, you get the worst over with right away. It's like tearing off a Band-Aid—if you do it fast, it doesn't hurt."

Lilly rolled her eyes. "The last time you took off a Band-Aid, you screamed so loud your dad called 911," she said. She turned to Miley. "Ask for the good news first. Then you'll already be happy when you hear the bad news. Trust me, it will soften the blow."

"How about no news and we all get to go back to bed?" Jackson grumbled, spearing another pancake.

"What'll it be, bud?" Mr. Stewart asked. "Your call."

"Bad news . . . no, wait, wait!" Miley squeezed her eyes tight, crossed her fingers, and finally blurted out: "Good news! I want the good news first!"

"Okay," her dad said. "Here goes. The Breakpoint Surf Series is coming to Malibu—"

"The Breakpoint Surf Series?" Lilly jumped to her feet, her eyes sparkling with excitement. "Miley, that's fantastic! Fantastic, stupendous, *awesome* good news! Why, you ask?"

"Okay," Miley said agreeably. "Why?"

"Because the top competitor in the Breakpoint Surf Series is none other than"—Lilly paused before yelling the last two words—"Talen Wright!"

"Talen Wright?" Miley yelled back. "No!"

"Yes!"

"No!"

"Yes!"

She and Lilly started jumping up and down, squealing with delight. After a few moments, Miley realized that her father, Jackson, and Oliver were all staring at them in complete bewilderment.

"Who in tarnation are you girls talking about?" her dad asked.

"Talen Wright!" Miley explained.

Still nothing but blank faces. Miley spared one pitying glance for their ignorance and set out to enlighten them. "He's this Australian guy—"

"Who happens to be one of the top surfers in the world!" Lilly interrupted, too excited to be quiet.

"Even though he's only sixteen!" Miley rushed on. "Plus, he's totally—"

"—totally—" Lilly said.

"Cute!" they finished together.

Then they looked at each other and squealed again.

"Huh." Mr. Stewart didn't look convinced. "To me, it sounds more like he's totally, totally trouble."

But Miley wasn't listening. She had developed a major crush on Talen a few months ago when he was chosen to be on the cover of *Teen Talk* magazine's Gorgeous Guys issue. She had instantly subscribed to *Teen Talk* to make sure she got the latest Talen Wright news, had started watching surfing competitions on TV, and daydreamed constantly about meeting him. And now, he was coming to Malibu!

"Talen Wright," she murmured to herself. Even his name sounded cute.

Oliver scowled and took an extralarge bite of pancake. "What kind of name is Talen, anyway?" he muttered.

But Miley didn't hear him because her

father was trying to get back to his main point. "As I was saying," he went on, "the good news is, there's going to be a big concert in two weeks at the end of the surfing contest. And the organizers want Hannah Montana to be the headliner!"

Miley and Lilly just stared at him, too stunned to speak.

What both Lilly and Oliver knew, and most of the world did not, was that Miley Stewart was not a typical high school student. She had a secret identity as Hannah Montana, one of the biggest pop stars in the world. Sometimes Miley had a hard time juggling her two lives, but most of the time she felt, as the title of her hit song said, that she had "The Best of Both Worlds."

Like, right now, for example.

Lilly found her voice first. "Miley," she whispered. "You are so, so lucky."

"I know." Miley nodded, her eyes wide.

"If you give a concert for the surf series,

you could actually get to meet Talen Wright." Lilly held out her arm. "Look! I have goose-bumps!"

"Me, too!" Miley squealed.

Oliver pushed his empty plate away. He had been thinking about having another pan-cake or two, but somehow he wasn't that hun-gry anymore. "Big deal. So you're going to meet some sunburned surfer dude. I bet he uses words like 'gnarly' and 'cowabunga.' I bet he tells people he's 'stoked.'"

"Who cares about his conversation?" Lilly sighed, a faraway look in her eyes.

"Who cares if he can even talk," Miley agreed.

Her dad cleared his throat meaningfully. Miley's smile dimmed. She didn't know any-one else who could clear his throat in such an ominous way.

"Okay," she said. "The good news is way too good to be true. So, lay it on me. What's the bad news?"

"I had a talk with your principal. It seems you got a little behind in your schoolwork from going on the road for those concerts last winter. Specifically, you got a little behind in English class." He gave her a serious look. "Apparently, you were supposed to keep a journal all semester. Ring a bell?"

"Oh, right." Miley's toes curled guiltily. Of course she had *meant* to keep up with her journal, but somehow all the rehearsals and costume fittings and talk show appearances kept getting in the way. And then she had started putting off one assignment with the idea that she would double up the next week. Before long, she had fallen so far behind that she had stopped even thinking about the class because it made her so anxious. She shuddered just thinking about it. "Maybe just a *little.*"

"Uh-huh."

"But the teacher didn't take off many points!" she went on quickly. "I just got a B instead of a B plus. That's still a very decent grade. Most parents would be proud."

But her father shook his head. "We talked about this before your last tour, Miley," he said. "I'm willing to let you miss a few days of school here and there if you keep up with *all* your homework. But I don't want you to get used to taking shortcuts, even if your grades are still okay."

Miley bit her lip. "I know, I know," she said. "I'll do better next year, I promise."

"Actually," Mr. Stewart said, "you'll do better *this* year. Turns out your principal came up with a way for you to make up that work. . . ."